THE
DECOMPOSITION
OF
JACK

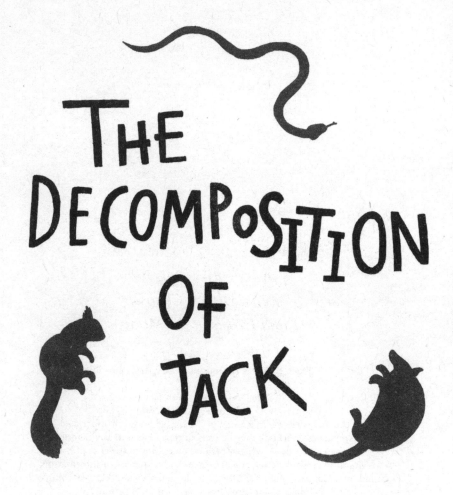

THE DECOMPOSITION OF JACK

KRISTIN O'DONNELL TUBB

KATHERINE TEGEN BOOKS
An Imprint of HarperCollins Publishers

Katherine Tegen Books is an imprint of HarperCollins Publishers.

The Decomposition of Jack
Copyright © 2022 by Kristin O'Donnell Tubb

Library of Congress Control Number: 2021953554
ISBN 978-0-06-321226-8

Typography by David DeWitt
22 23 24 25 26 PC/LSCH 10 9 8 7 6 5 4 3 2 1
❖
First Edition

For the Jacks in my life: Dad and Son

SCRAPE OR WAVE

When Mom offers me the option of scraping the roadkill off the highway or waving the cars around, I've learned to just suck it up and scrape. You get scowled at when you wave the cars around. You get honked at and swerved at. You get recognized.

But the scraping? You can keep your head down. And if it's cold, like today, you can tuck all but your eyes into your scarf. Sure, the folks in Abington likely know it's me out there with the snow shovel and bucket when they see my mom diverting traffic. But they can't look me in the eyes. I can't stand it when they look me in the eyes.

It's the pity. In their eyes. I don't like being pitied.

Because (a) I don't deserve it. They don't know the real story. And (b) who wants pity? Just the word is uncomfortable, like underwear stuck in someplace tight.

"Almost done, Jack?" Mom yells over her shoulder.

"Uh-huh," I answer through a pinched-off nose. This possum's been dead just a few hours. The bloat hasn't yet set in, and there's only a handful of flesh flies buzzing around.

The possum is heavier than I expect when I heft it off the pavement with the snow shovel. Much heavier. I'm guessing he had been maybe four years old, based on his size. Pretty rare.

I dump the possum into one of those huge paint buckets you get at the Home Depot. His body plunks into it with a crunching, smooshing sound. Bile rises in my throat. That noise gets me every time. Maggots, I can handle. Protruding bones, puddles of blood, strewn intestines—all okay. But the sound of the carcass echoing against the walls of a bucket, the stench of decay poofing up like a tiny green mushroom cloud—I still want to hurl.

"Easy, Jack!" Mom shouts. "You don't want to destroy its—"

HOOOOONNNNKKKK!

Mom's complaints about my roadkill undertaking skills are drowned out by another ticked-off motorist. I snap the lid onto the paint bucket.

But before we go: a roadside memorial fit for an old possum like this one. I scan the ditch next to the highway. There's a patch of dandelion pushing through a crack in the pavement as it tumbles down into the ditch. That dandelion is a survivor like this possum was. The flowers have turned to fluff and they're scraggly, patchy, which kinda reminds me of the rounded rump of this old fella. I pluck the weed and place it gently where the possum once was.

I always feel like I should say something profound in these moments, but I've never come up with anything that sounds right. Something to maybe usher these animals into the Big After. But it's hard to come up with something poetic when you don't know what After looks like. I shiver. "Sorry you had to go," I mumble at last.

I hoist the paint bucket and the shovel and head toward our beat-up station wagon.

The hatch of the wagon groans open. "Mom, there's nowhere to put this."

Mom waves away my hint that we leave this one behind. "Just shove some of the groceries aside."

I sigh and cram the bucket holding a dead possum inside our car, next to the ground beef, then join Mom in the front seat.

"What a score!" Mom says, blowing on her glove-less hands. She whips out her phone. I know she's logging on to iNaturalist.com and recording where and when—the exact spot, the exact time—we found our meaty little friend. I'll call him Gutsy. It's been a while since we've had a Gutsy.

Mom cranks the car. "I love this road! Chock full of specimens!" She bounces a little on the springy, wide car seat, and I can't help but smile. She's like a kid getting a present when she finds a fresh new hunk of animal carcass on the side of the road.

The Tennessee hills fly by while Mom rattles off her favorite finds from this stretch of highway. "Remember that small buck, Jack? Two points, I think. Wow. He was something else. Almost never got him home, ha! Thank goodness for bungee cords. Roof is still dented in. And the fox, remember? That red coat. Amazing. And, oh, the armadillos! Still can't get past the fact they've made their way over the—"

Mom slams on the brakes. I jerk forward against the seat belt. Mom's nostrils twitch. It makes me think of blowflies. Those little pests can smell death up to ten miles away.

Then, the smell hits me, too. There is no mistaking that smell.

"No, Mom," I say, shaking my head. "We can't put

that in our car. Plus, we already found one today. We don't need a—"

"Skunk!" Mom says. She puts the car into park and hops out before I can finish.

Mom is hunched over, her sparkly, excited eyes scanning left and right for the skunk. I see it, the pile of black-white-red fur ahead, but I don't point it out. Maybe she'll miss it. Maybe she'll—

"There!" she says, and bounces on her toes. "Scrape or wave, Jack?"

I crawl out of the car. Eesh—the skunk musk is so strong it makes my eyes water, even here, ten feet away. No way I'm scraping that mess up. Nope. I'll take my chances waving. I hand Mom the shovel.

"Chicken," she says with a wink.

"If it was a chicken, I'd scrape it."

Mom laughs, a sort of snort-giggle that makes me laugh, too.

She jogs over to the carcass and begins whistling. It's her trick for not breathing in through her nose. I haven't learned how to do it yet. I still dab a bit of Vicks VapoRub under my nose every time I have to peel a carcass off the road. It smells like being stabbed in the sinuses with ten thousand pine needles, but it mostly wipes out the stench.

I turn to face the oncoming traffic. My breath puffs

in the cold air, and I think about how each one of those puffs proves I'm alive. *Puff puff puff.* Molecules that were once a part of me, now in the air, fading away.

I wave two cars around. They swing wide, passing me, our swagger wagon, and Mom and her treasure. Questioning looks, but nothing mean. Maybe we can get out of here with relative ease. I turn to check on our progress.

"Whoo! This little stinker is a real prize, Jack!" my mom yells. "Young. Most of the entrails intact. And just wait till you see the gams on him!" I shake off a smile.

Beebeep! Beep!

The friendly little horn toot makes me jump.

"Everything okay, soldier?" The voice booms out of a tiny Lexus next to me. Soldier. He's referring to my camo pants.

"Yes, sir. We just—"

My voice stops working when I lean down to eye level with the car. There, in the passenger seat, is a pair of Algebra Green eyes. I call it that color—Algebra Green—because these particular eyes hang in the head that sits diagonally behind me in Algebra. The Algebra Green eyes, I avoid at all costs.

"You need to use my cell phone or something?" her dad asks. "Call a tow?"

I shake my head, but my stupid voice is still MIA.

My mom walks up just then, shows me the yellow bucket that reeks to high heaven. "Got him, Jack. Now, let's go eat lunch."

THE WORLD IN A 3 X 5 SQUARE

S*creee-BLAM!*
The screen door into the backyard bangs shut, but that doesn't bother the buzzards hanging out there one bit. They're used to it.

I walk right up to a gaggle of them—I don't know if they really are called a gaggle, but *gag* seems to fit— and stomp my foot. "Go on! Get outta here!"

Two of the greasy birds hop a few feet away and peck at another carcass. The third sizes me up with beady black eyes.

I'm not mad. He's just having a little snack. Doing what his bird-brain instincts tell him to do. He doesn't know he's eating Mom's experiments.

I sigh. "C'mon, dude. Get out of here." I lean in

close and whisper, "Don't make me call Mom. You know what she'll do." I drag my finger across my neck, "*Kkkk-kk-kkk,*" then point at the bird. "You'll be lying right there next to them, bub."

This is hyperbole, of course. Mom would never disrupt the natural cycle of decay. In fact, she'd be ticked that I'm chasing them off right now. But I'm betting these buzzards don't know that.

The buzzard pecks at the decomposing rabbit—Cottontail—one last time. He hooks a string of entrails with his beak. He lifts one mighty claw and slices the ligament from the carcass with a *snap*. The bird tosses back his head and swallows the string of meat down his gullet before flapping away.

My friend André shouts from inside the house. "Are they gone?"

I smile. "Yep. No more big, scary birdies."

Screee-BLAM!

"Don't make fun. Those birds could peck an eye out."

"Yep. They do every day." I sweep my hand over our backyard, littered with picked-over animal carcasses and patches of dead brown grass.

André's face curls and his whole body convulses. "Sick. Meat-eating birds? An evolutionary step gone wrong, if you ask me."

I look up at the birds, now circling wide and low

overhead. There isn't much of a difference between me and them, as far as I can see. We both stay alive by scraping animal carcasses off the highway. But of course I don't say that.

I lift the bucket I'd hauled into the backyard. "Want to see him?"

André's eyes light up and he whips out his sketch pad. "He's big, you say?"

"And pretty intact."

"Cool."

"Drumroll, please."

André gives me a drumroll by smacking the palms of his hands on his legs.

"Introducing," I announce, "the Acosta family's newest pet, Gutsy!"

The possum lolls out of the bucket and lands on our lush grass, quivering like jelly. André swallows and jerks his head to the side.

"What's the matter?" A teasing tone sings through my voice. I smile.

"Whew," André says, lifting the collar of his shirt over his nose. "Another possum?"

"They're not exactly speed demons. We see these old guys a lot."

André shudders. "Guess I'll get started."

While I rope off the area around Gutsy the possum, André plops in the grass and starts sketching. The point of his pencil sweeps over the paper and leaves a thick mark here, a thin stroke there. Before I know it, I am looking at the beginning panels of his next *Zombie Zoo* comic.

I stand there, absorbing it, like I do every time I watch André create his comic. To bring something to life, instead of watching it fade into death? It's like watching a movie run backward to me.

But there is work to be done, so I tear myself away from André's zombies. I turn on our construction-grade tablet and pull up the roadkill database Mom designed. Might as well start with Cottontail. Or what's left of him.

Subject—Cottontail: male Eastern cottontail rabbit
Estimated age—9 months
Day—11
Date—November 6
Rainfall—1.2 centimeters
Sun exposure—very little
Current temperature—40 degrees F
Stage of decomposition—stage 3, active decay/black
   putrefaction
Insects present—blowfly and fly larvae, maggots, beetles,
   parasitoid wasps
Odors—strong (linger-in-your-nostrils-after-you've-stepped-
   away strong). Methane and ammonia.

Notes—bloat and beginning stages of discoloration—yellowy
fur. Orifices no longer pink but rimmed with green and
purple.

I pause, then add a smiley face at the bottom: ☺.
Mom could use more smiley faces in her day. The faces
she usually sees are grimaces, faces showing the last-
words shock of *Oh no, a car!*

Next row of the spreadsheet, next rotting body.
Giggles, I call her. A raccoon. And back and forth
through the yard, collecting stats and avoiding roped-
off graveyards and piles of buzzard poop. A rat. Three
frogs. Two snakes. Several possums. A deer. Six or
seven squirrels. A polecat, all nine lives used up.

"I gotta dash," André shouts across the yard. He
drops his sketchbook into a backpack. "Going to the
Sugar Shack. Wanna go?"

I shake my head and cross the yard to him, weaving
through the tiny roped-off areas containing bones and
guts and poo. "Can't. More work to do."

"Ditch it. I really miss hanging out with you, man.
All you do lately is work, work, work." He marches
as he says this, like I'm in the army or something. The
Splatoon Platoon. I laugh.

"Yeah, I can't. My mom really needs my help."

André nods, squints. The look he gives when I'm
about to get one of his voices. "You're a good kid,

kid," he says in his best New York accent. "One a da best."

"You just love me for my roadkill."

He punches me on the arm and changes to a fluttery, high-pitched voice. "And your buzzard-chasing skills. You have *ahhhhmazing* buzzard-chasing skills."

André bows and tips his Titans hat to the dozen bodies wasting away in my backyard. "Carry on, carrion!" He hops on his bike and coasts down the hill into town.

Not thirty seconds later, three more bikes zip by. "Hey, Roadkill Kid!" one of them yells. I know the voice coming from beneath that spiky black bike helmet. It's Cameron Totallyawful from my Earth Science class. (Totallyawful isn't his real last name, of course, but Totallyawful is definitely accurate.) As they pass, I hear Cameron say, "*That* dude's not going to the Sugar Shack. Guy's got a whole bunch of yummy guts cooking in his backyard. *Mmm-MMM!*"

His two cronies laugh. Is it bad that I chuckle when one of them hits a patch of gravel and his bike wheels skid wildly? He doesn't crash, but he squeals like a squirrel escaping an oncoming semi.

So they're headed to the Sugar Shack, too. Right. I've never been. Nobody there wants to watch the Roadkill Kid scarf down a double cheeseburger. Folks always seem surprised that I'm not a vegetarian. For the record, the only thing I cannot eat are gummy worms. *Ugh!* Can*not* do it.

Cameron started calling me the Roadkill Kid when he spotted me scraping a groundhog off Highway 98 last month. This is never a role I wanted, of course. It's a role I inherited, thanks to my dad leaving. *Running away,* actually. But, hey, those animals squished on the side of the road didn't get what *they* wanted either, so I don't complain. And at least Mom has one strict rule when it comes to collecting carrion—absolutely no pets. No dogs, no cats, no domesticated rabbits— nothing that would live inside a home. They mess up the data, but also, it's easier when you're dealing with a mole with no name. Until I name her Princess Elsa.

Just as I finish up my notes, I see something move out of the corner of my eye. Things that move are studied in my backyard, because they're a part of the decomposi- tion cycle Mom's so interested in. It was just a flash, a zip through the tall grass, over the fence, into the trees. I don't really want to study whatever this thing is right now—*Super Smash Brothers* isn't going to play itself. I run my fingers along the chain-link fence as I walk the perimeter of the yard—*tinginginginginging*—a warn- ing to the thing that moves.

Whatever I saw is gone. But it was something, because there, in a patch of mud, is a huge paw print, at least four inches across. It is smooth and curvy and deeper in the front, like the moving thing pushed off from this spot in a leap.

And it is warm. That surprises me, for some reason. My fingers flutter just over the paw print, over the hollows in the mud. I don't want to touch it. This is movement, frozen.

I need to keep it that way. Preserve it. I consider digging it up, like a slab of rock containing a fossil, but I know that once the mud dries, the slab will crumble.

The heat is leaving the paw print quickly, like a ghost. And once the clouds break open and dump cold rain, I will lose the paw forever. I dash into the house and grab Dad's old camera. I blow on it once, twice to get rid of the dust, run back outside, and snap a photo.

This is going to sound crazy—even crazier than a kid who helps his mom scrape and study roadkill—but the sun is setting just as I snap the photo, and the crystals in the mud sparkle just so, and the curves of the paw soak in shadows like tiny, dark crescent moons, and the grass bows and prays around the edges of the photo, blurry and waving, and the whole picture looks like magic.

Mom comes to the screen door. "What's all the hubbub? One of Ms. Zachary's dogs try to dig under again?"

I look at the viewer on the back of the camera until it fades. If I show this to Mom, she'll find a way to turn it into an experiment. I don't want to analyze this creature's every meal, every pile of dung. This animal is stealthy and sly, and she goes unnoticed, mostly. I know how that feels.

No, I want the magic a little longer.

"Nothing," I say. My stomach twists, a feeling I'm not used to since my stomach is made of steel. "Just some interesting maggots."

Mom smiles. "Every maggot is interesting! The recyclers of the universe, those little guys! Long live maggots!" She laughs at her joke—maggots only live about eight days—flips her dish towel, and marches into the house.

I bring the picture back up on the screen. Amazing, even though it's just mud and grass and an animal print. There is something satisfying about whittling the world down to one three-by-five square. I brought this photo to life, like André does with his comics. A thrill shoots through me, like the feeling of jumping off a swing at its highest point.

I place the toe of my Converse over the paw print and squish, burying the print under sneaker tread. Just in case the rain doesn't erase it all the way.

"Come back tomorrow," I whisper into the trees. "She won't be here then."

3

ANOTHER HAM

I type "paw print four inches wild Tennessee" and upload the photo I took.

Google returns: *cougar*

Cougar? In Tennessee?

No way. Spotting a cougar in Tennessee is like saying you saw Bigfoot or Elvis. It's a bobcat, maybe. That has to be it.

"Murck! Mirl you mer mrat?"

I tug my gaming headphones off my ears. "What?"

"The door, Jack! See who it is, please?"

I swivel out of my chair and tumble downstairs. By the time I open the door, the only thing I see is a blue Chevy van turning the corner. I blink, look down.

There it is, on our doormat that says, "If you're pizza, Amazon, or Ryan Gosling, I'm home." It's a big lump of gold tinfoil in a plastic bag. A ham.

My face burns like that time I visited Hilton Head Island and wore only 30 SPF.

"Jack? Who is it?" Mom yells from the backyard.

I scoop up the lump and stomp through the house.

The screen door in the back screeches. I heft the bag. It's heavy. And drippy. "They left us another ham."

Mom squints in my direction, shades her eyes. She sighs.

"*Mom*. You have got to tell those ladies we're okay."

"Jack, I have. They're just being charitable."

"*Mom*. They think we *eat roadkill*."

Mom swallows past the lump in her throat. "They mean well, Jack."

"They didn't do this when Dad was still here! You gathered roadkill for years before that."

Mom nods. "And isn't that just a lesson in how the world sees women in science? They understood your dad being one of the world's preeminent road-kill researchers. They don't get that I was always his partner."

She's being modest. She's always been the lead researcher. I suspect for her that was the hardest part of Dad leaving us a couple months ago: she had to rebuild

18

her research process from the ground up. (Literally the ground. Mushrooms and maggots and all.)

Mom's research focuses on the decomposition process: life into death. Dad looks at what happens to the soil and plants after a carcass decomposes: death into life. And if *that* doesn't describe their personalities, I don't know what does.

I watched Mom and Dad's marriage skid through each phase of the decomposition process together: autolysis, rigor mortis, bloat, active decay, advanced decay, skeletonized. R.I.P.

That's why I try to help her so much. She can't lose Dad *and* her roadkill.

Mom gets paid to study dead wildlife through a grant from the University of Tennessee. How death and decay become lushness and life. When Dad left, when he ran away, we lost the lushness and life part. But we couldn't lose the grant money. And we're coming up on a big deadline for Mom—she reports all her data at the end of every year, and that's in just a few weeks. So, I help. I'm not sure I understand it all, what we measure and snip and clip and observe, but I like food and clothes and roofs, so I help. No one told me I needed to, but it was obvious I should.

Mom hasn't budged from her spot next to Rosebud, our newest skunk. I huff. Lift the bag of ham again.

"What should I do with this?"

"Put it in the fridge for now."

I narrow my eyes. Mom usually marches right back to our church and kindly returns the food the ladies' guild leaves for us, explaining that we're *fine*, everything's *fine*.

I shove the ham into our fridge, and dozens of bottles and sauces clink out of the way. My stomach grumbles.

I'm not eating that ham.

TO THE VERY END

Get up, Jack. We're going to church today."

It's the following morning, and it's sunny and cold. I sit up quickly, rub my eyes. We don't make it to church every week, but I love it when we go. My favorite color—Algebra Green—is there.

Mom leans back into the doorway of my bedroom. "And hey! Thanks for the chocolate, Jack. Godiva! I feel like the queen, eating that fancy stuff!"

She chuckles and pretends to sip tea with her pinky raised. I smile down at my huge fuzzy Chewbacca slippers. I had to trade Joey Fillipelli my whole peanut-butter-and-banana sandwich for that one chocolate, but it made Mom smile.

We pile into the swagger wagon, wave off the flies, and head to church. As we pull into the parking lot, I tuck my too-long hair behind my ears. "I need a haircut, Mom."

Mom has slammed the car into park. "Mmmm-hmmm," she says, fishing around on the floorboard behind my seat. Mom tosses her large straw purse over her shoulder, adjusts her hair, and in we go.

I feel her before I see her. Algebra Green. Zoe is her name. Doesn't that name sound like someone with a great smile? I grin a bit, make contact out of the corner of my eye, and work up the courage to give her a wave. She waves back, and I feel like Stage Four Decomposition: entrails turning inside out.

Mom marches up to the fourth row and we sit. We stand, we sing. Our small church has floor-to-ceiling stained-glass windows, and the slant of colorful light makes my finger twitch. I want to take a photograph here, inside this rainbow. I want to capture the feeling of slow light and soft color and inside-out entrails.

"We thank you for giving generously," the deacon says. The brass plate passes from hand to hand, and people gently toss in slips of paper and coins. Mom reaches for her massive purse.

The brass plate gets to me. I twist toward Mom.

"Hold it tight," she whispers, and she plunks in a

huge lump of gold tinfoil. Before I realize what she's done, she takes the plate from me and passes it along.

The ham!

I'm going to sizzle and burn into tiny bits of carbon and dissipate into the universe, right here in pew four.

That ham gets fondled and sniffed by twenty more sets of hands before it makes its way back to the usher. It's heavy and drippy and smelly, too. The usher blinks, looks around, unsure what to do with a ham in the collection plate.

At last, she plucks it out of the plate and tucks it into the crook of her arm like a football. I hope it doesn't get ham juices all over her nice shirt.

"Mom, let's go," I whisper. Every eye in church is on that ham. I sink in the pew, not daring to look back to see gold tinfoil reflected in Zoe's eyes.

"We'll stay to the very end," she whispers back.

To the very end.

That's Stage Five Decomposition: just a fur pelt, a few bones, and some scraggly teeth left behind in the mud.

Sounds about right.

COMPOSERS VERSUS
DECOMPOSERS

We get in the car and shoo away the flies. I turn up the radio. Mom turns down the radio.

"Did you hear that Matilda woman as we were leaving? 'Who would study roadkill?' I'll tell you who, Matilda!"

"I love this song," I try. I turn up the radio again. Mom turns down the radio again.

"Conservation experts, Matilda, that's who. Soil experts. Wildlife experts. Civil engineers. Environmentalists. Artists. DNA experts. People who work for museums. Matilda, if you only *knew* how much of your life was built around the sciences you never even think about!"

Why isn't Matilda here listening to all this instead of me? I envy Matilda. I consider turning up the radio one more time. Instead, I snap a hand forward, catch a fly. It feels buzzy and odd in my fist. I roll down the window and release it.

"Nice," Mom says, but it doesn't break her stride. "They've made improvements to organic fertilizer based on my research, *Matilda*. They've built roads differently to keep *you* safe. They've even used my research to solve crimes, *Matilda*. Dead bodies, missing bodies—we're all roadkill to a turkey buzzard."

I hate it when she talks like this. I know what she's trying to say—that our bodies are miracles but they are our temporary home. But she never says it quite like that.

I really miss Dad at moments like this. I don't miss them *together,* but Dad could always talk her out of one of these spirals. What would he say?

They had this running joke about the world's greatest composers versus the world's greatest decomposers. Bach, Beethoven, and Mozart versus buzzards, bugs, and maggots. "Who? Would? *Win?*" they'd bellow, and we'd all laugh, because the decomposers always win in the end. Just ask Beethoven's bones.

"Matilda wouldn't know a turkey buzzard from Tchaikovsky," I say.

It does the trick. Mom tosses her head back and

laughs. She turns the radio up. "You love this song."

I smile.

Spiral successfully squashed.

Mom slams on the brakes.

"Jack, look! A squirrel!"

I think for a moment of that movie with the dog, the one who gets so easily distracted: *Squirrel!*

That's not what she means, though. She's already pulling on her coat and hopping out of our car.

"Scrape or wave, bud?"

WELCOME TO THE ROADKILL GARDEN

P*ing!*

Dad: Sorry I can't swing by today after all, bud—packing for a road trip to Arizona. Leave tomorrow. Rattlers, BABY! Hope you're taking good care of your mom. Love you!

His text is followed by a bunch of stupid emojis: A sun. A snake. A car. All those ridiculous cartoon pictures—are they supposed to cheer me up or something?

I'm scheduled to spend every other weekend at Dad's apartment, but the last two times he's been traveling for work. I look away from my phone. A road trip to Arizona? And he leaves tomorrow? Adults think kids are so stupid. You can't plan a trip like that in a day. How long has he known about it?

When the car stops, I hop out and head to the backyard. "I'll take the squirrel," I say. "Show him the ropes. Introduce him to the other pets. Make him feel welcome."

Mom smiles. "You know the drill. Tag the ankle. Type of animal, date, and—"

"Place of kill, got it," I say. "Should I swab it, too?" I hate that part, reaching a Q-tip into all sorts of animal orifices.

"Nah, I'll do it in a bit." Mom ruffles my hair, which is weird because I'm almost as tall as she is.

"Haircut," I say, pointing to the hair she just ruffled. I can feel it standing on end. "I need."

"Hmmmm," Mom says, scanning the cloudy sky.

There's this rumor that hair and nails keep growing even after death. Dad told me it wasn't true, that it just looks that way because the skin shrinks back.

Geez. Why do I know this stuff?

"Hey, Mom. Do you maybe want to, uh, work on some Legos later?" Inside, spread out all over our dining room table, is a half-completed AT-AT. Gray Legos are everywhere. It's going to be awesome if I can ever finish it. It's been weeks since Mom and I worked on it. Dad didn't have the patience for Lego kits, but Mom and I love them.

Doesn't. Dad *doesn't* have the patience for Lego kits. I don't know why I'm thinking of him in the past tense.

Mom blinks and shakes her head, like she's waking up. "Can't honey. Sorry. The squirrel. I want a tongue sample, too. The coloring on this one's interesting."

I shiver. Tongue samples are the *worst.* Like clipping toenails, but instead? Tongue. *Ugh.* But it's a great way to get a DNA sample.

I round the corner of the house and unlatch the metal gate. The stench of twelve rotting corpses hits me, but I'll get used to the stink pretty fast. I hit the shed first and grab a plastic zip tie and a metal tag. They look like dog tags, but they're soft enough to write on. They bend under the weight of a pencil point.

Squirrel

November 14

DOR Mullens Mill Road

I pause, then add, "Chuckles."

Next, I shuffle Chuckles around inside the plastic grocery bag he's in, until I can access an ankle.

Zip!

Chuckles has new jewelry.

I step gingerly around Mom's stinking piles of work and find a piece of yard away from all the other barren brown spots where carcasses rot. Chuckles gets a spot on the far left, near the woodpile.

"R.I.P. Chuck." He tumbles out of the grocery bag and hits the ground with a sickening bone-crunch. "Welcome to the Roadkill Garden."

Mom hoists open the kitchen window, yells from inside: "Tacos for lunch! They'll be ready soon."

There's a green plastic chair in the taller grass at the back of our lot, near the tree line. I plop into it and try not to think about how far away Arizona is and how much rattlesnake venom it would take to level a 185-pound adult. I shake my head to clear the thought.

I tilt my face to the sun. My breath is clouds. All the poets and authors write about October, but give me the light of November any day. It's the color of pink lemonade.

I like it when the weather gets colder. The roadkill is better. Preserved, like in a freezer. Summer roadkill is the *worst*. Try scraping an armadillo off a 120-degree black tar road. *Whew!*

I exhale. My breath disappears.

My skin crawls.

I am being watched.

I look across the expanse of yard, over so many patches of dead grass. None of those critters have eyes anymore, except Chuckles. And I give him about six more hours with his, tops.

I turn slowly toward the trees. Look up.

It's there.

Between the yellow leaves.

Yellow eyes.

A huge cat, sitting in a tree.

Her body is in shadows, hidden by a tangle of limbs and leaves. It's hard to tell how big she is.

"Hi," I whisper. My breath lifts toward her.

She doesn't move. Doesn't blink.

She could leap down on me and add me to the list of critters in this backyard in a heartbeat.

Speaking of heartbeats, mine's in my throat.

In my stomach.

In my teeth.

Screeee-BLAM!

"Jack, dude, your mom's taco game is *sick*! She's got chicken and steak and—"

The whole tree bends and rustles when she leaps away, farther into the forest. Leaves rain down.

And a long, graceful tail arcs behind her.

"What was *that*?" André asks. I can see him gulp from here.

"That," I say, realizing how weird and hollow my voice sounds through my pounding pulse, "was a cougar."

"André the Giant, have a seat," Mom says. She offers him a chair with a small kick to its leg while holding a plate of tacos.

"André the Giant, see, that's funny," he says with a wink at me. "It's funny because I'm *short*, Jack."

"I get it," I mumble. I'm still looking out the window. "Ha."

André shakes his head, grabs four tacos as they pass him by. "Well, I'm glad that cougar didn't take you out, dude. That thing was *close*." He shudders.

The plate of tacos plonks to the table.

"Cougar?"

My lips mash together. For some reason, I don't know why, I still don't want Mom to know about this cougar. Not just yet anyways. I like it being my secret. The pet I can't have because, well, my mom collects roadkill.

It was magic, locking eyes with that big cat. She moved like the wind moves sand.

"It wasn't a cougar," I say, boring a hole through the taco plate with my eyes. "It was . . . a bobcat."

It wasn't a bobcat. Bobcats don't have tails. That's what the *bob* in bobcat means: bobbed tail.

That cat's tail was as long as a rattlesnake.

"Ah! Makes sense. We can't have a cougar. That would be a data nightmare. We'd definitely have to chase off something like that."

Chase her off? I knew there was a reason I didn't want to tell Mom about this cat.

André and Mom cut it up, and I'm slowly brought back to earth by their laughter. They're currently debating which eighties rap group was superior: Run DMC or the Beastie Boys. I love André and Mom's friendship. They talk so easy, and not about death and decay at all. I don't know how he does it.

The longer I sit there and listen to them laugh, the more I begin to doubt what I saw. Was it a tail? Maybe it was a limb swaying in the wind, swaying under the weight of her leap?

My finger twitches.

I want a picture of that cat.

A STINKING TRAIL CAMERA

What I need is a trail camera. But I can't ask Mom for one of those. The good ones with night vision are over a hundred dollars. I've seen how she bites her nails paying the bills.

It's gross enough that my mom, who touches oh-so-very-much roadkill, bites her fingernails. I can't add my greedy grossness on top of that.

We hit a pothole and bounce off our green plastic bench.

"Earth to Jack," André is saying. I blink at him.

"Check it out—new *Zombie Zoo*."

"Well, give it here!"

I glance over the panels with a smile. In the

first scene, a small animal hunches in a corner. It's adorable—big bushy tail, tiny fuzzy ears, huge kawaii eyes, the whole bit. Second panel: Two kids see it, and one says, "Is that a sugar glider?" "Awwww!" coos the second kid.

Next panel: they lean in close.

Next panel: closer . . .

Cut to the sugar glider springing at them, this time zombiefied: all drool and ooze and dead eyes. He is, of course, shouting "BRAAAIIIINNNNNSSSSS!"

Then: One kid running in circles with a zombie sugar glider spread across his face, blood spurting every-where. The other kid screams, "AHHHHHHHH!" while crouched and peeking at the massacre through his hands mashed over his eyes.

Final panel: The attacked kid lies on the floor, the free kid trying to pull the leech-like sugar glider off his face. The free kid has a foot on the attacked kid's chest, and the sugar glider's legs are *stretched* while the kid pulls. The free kid says, "No one will EVER BELIEVE THIS. Sugar gliders can TALK!"

I laugh and smile at André. "You're going to be a published cartoonist one day."

"Syndication is the goal there, my man," André says, tucking his sketch pad into his backpack. "Jim Davis's *Garfield* comics were in 2,570 newspapers worldwide.

He's in the *Guinness Book of World Records* for it."

André leans back, and the plastic bus seat makes a fart noise. "I'm going to be in 2,571."

"Are there even that many newspapers?"

André shrugs, then sits bolt upright. "But! Here's where it'll all start."

He scrambles through his Under Armour backpack, removing several balled-up math worksheets. Empty packets of gum. A dog-eared copy of *Black Boy Joy*. A set of earbuds with a cord that looks like it will never untangle.

André gets to a wad of newspaper. He clutches it briefly against his chest and inhales. I squeeze back a smile; the gesture reminds me of when Dad reads a poem he really loves. He'll inhale deeply, like breathing it in will help lock the poem inside himself.

I wonder if Dad still does that. I wouldn't know.

"*The Gator Gazette*," André says, smoothing out our school newspaper on the bus seat between us. (There is no apparent explanation as to why a middle school in Tennessee has a gator as its mascot. Every Abington Middle student has wondered this.)

"Check it out, dude." He jabs his finger at an ad on the front page of the paper.

Calling All Cartoonists! We need your art HERE! Submit five samples to Ms. Sergio before winter break.

One cartoonist will be selected. The winner's cartoons will run in the next several issues of The Gator Gazette!

I blink. "What? This is perfect for you."

André's smile widens. "Right? Bud, I need your help picking samples. You'll do that?"

"Absolutely," I say. I grin at him. "You're going to be a published cartoonist."

"Yeah, I am."

I smile. I put my forehead against the cool window. I'm happy for André. It must be nice to have a goal like that. All I want is a stinking trail camera.

WHY, VOICE BOX? WHY?!

So, about those Algebra-Green eyes. They would more accurately be called Algebra-and-Earth-Science Green, because those are the two classes Zoe and I have together. But I first noticed Zoe's eyes in math class, so . . . Algebra Green.

Today Zoe is wearing a T-shirt that matches her eyes and says "There Is No Planet B." Her hair falls long and straight by the sides of her face, and it reminds me of the color of fox fur.

Alive fox fur.

Ms. Bennett raps her knuckles on her desk and adjusts her red cat-eye glasses. "Okay, Earthlings!" (She always calls us that. Because it's Earth Science class, I guess.) "Today we're going to pick the animal we'd like to study for our end-of-semester project!"

Ms. Bennett smiles huge and judders her hands like this is a big celebration. The class groans.

She ignores us. Teachers are amazing: they can ignore so many big things, but also notice the tiniest things, too.

"So. You know the rules, Earthlings. One! You can't pick an animal someone else has picked. And two! The animal has to be a part of Tennessee's ecosystem."

Ms. Bennett gets super jazzed about ecosystems.

"To make things fair, I'm going to draw names out of this jar, and that's when you tell me which animal you'd like to study."

She draws names, and the class rattles off animals:

"Ashvi?"

"Ornate box turtle."

"Jalen?"

"Eastern cottontail."

"Chloe?"

"Cottonmouth snake."

"Jack?"

I don't really hear her, because I'm looking down at my sheet of paper where I've written "raccoon." The Tennessee state animal. Also, a big yawn. I could tell you about raccoons inside and out, literally. I've

39

probably seen sixty of them turn into nothing but pairs of leathery clawed hands in my backyard.

"Jack?"

George, behind me, kicks my chair.

"Oh! Uh. Cougar."

What did I just say?! It slipped out before I could stop my mouth muscles from forming the words. Why, voice box? Why?!

Ms. Bennett's brow furrows and she looks over the top of her red cat-eye glasses. "Hmmm. Jack, I'm not so sure about your pick. Cougars are extinct in Tennessee."

Cameron Totallyawful guffaws and smacks the top of his desk. "You gotta be kidding me! If that ain't *the best*! The Roadkill Kid, picking up dead animals again!"

Several class members giggle.

"Cameron!" Ms. Bennett cuts in, lips pursed. "There's no need for that. And sit *up*, please."

Cameron removes his Vans from the back of the chair in front of him and flips his long brown bangs out of his eyes. "But seriously. Pick an alive animal for once, dude."

He flips his hair again. His twitchiness reminds me of when rigor mortis sets in, particularly in rodents. About four hours after an animal has died, rigor mortis makes a creature's muscles seize up, tighten, and even though they're dead, they *twitch*. It's creepy as all get out. Cameron's hair flip looks just like it.

Right then, Zoe's hand shoots into the air. "Pardon me, Ms. Bennett. I'd be very interested to hear what Jack finds. My environmentalist club says there is reason to believe that some western cougars have migrated back to this region over the last few years."

I mean, she's wearing a shirt that says "There Is No Planet B." I'm inclined to believe her.

Ms. Bennett must be, too. "Really? Well, then. That is interesting. And I suppose even if they are extinct, you can tell us why. I'll put you down for cougar, Jack."

Cameron and his awful friends all snort-laugh and whisper cougar jokes to each other. Ha-ha.

"Cameron? Your animal of choice?"

"Raccoon."

The animal selection continues, and when the bell rings, a piece of paper slides across my desk. I look up and gasp. Zoe!

"Check out these two websites for your research," she says, tapping the paper. "The first one is the state website. The big, official one. They say cougars are extinct. The second one is the state wildlife and game website. Still official, but they say the opposite. Interesting, don't you think?"

She pauses, arms crossed, and I realize I've been staring at her freckles and I got lost somewhere back at "The first one is . . ."

Zoe knocks a knuckle against the paper. "Anyway. Glad you picked this. I can't wait to see what you find."

I watch her and her hair and her freckles and her green eyes leave the room.

Can't wait to see what I find?

So far all I have is a paw print, a set of yellow eyes, and a tail. What I *think* is a tail. And Zoe is excited about what I might find?

No pressure, dude.

EASIER TO DENY THEY EXIST

The piece of paper Zoe gave me is sweaty and gross because I kept it in my fist jammed inside my pocket the whole way home. I wanted to make sure I didn't lose it, I guess. I'm glad the pencil didn't wash off.

I go to the big state website first. "The Eastern cougar was deemed extinct by the U.S. Fish and Wildlife Service in 2018." That was just a few years ago! An animal went *extinct* just a few years ago and we didn't hear all about it on the news and in school? This site declares without a doubt: no cougars have been spotted in Tennessee since the early 1900s. So, officially moved from "endangered" to "extinct."

There is a footnote on this website; its title is "The

Cost of Keeping an Animal 'Endangered.'" When I click through, though, it's just a bunch of numbers and tables and legal-sounding words.

Then I visit the website for the Tennessee Wildlife Resources Agency. It begins with a description of cougars: "Adults are large, sleek cats with small heads . . . ears are black and small and rounded . . . muzzle is white . . . long, cylindrical tails ranging in length from 20 to 30 inches . . ."

It says that cougars often walk hundreds of miles to find new territory, and they suspect cougars are moving here from the West. Western cougars—a different breed, but still, cougars in Tennessee. And hundreds of miles! I hate running one mile in gym class. Hundreds?

I don't get it. Why would one site say, *absolutely no cougars!* and another say, *ehhh maybe*?

I sit back for a second, and my gaming chair creaks. Why deny that cougars are here? Why not accept them . . . ? Why . . . ?

I sit up. My chair spins.

That footnote says why.

Cost.

I mean, if the state of Tennessee knows that a pride of cougars has made the trek here to call this place home, they would need to protect them, wouldn't they? They'd have to pass hunting and trapping laws, set up habitats, tell people about them—all sorts of stuff. They'd have to spend a lot of money on that kind of thing.

It's easier to deny they exist.

I bet the state is ignoring that cougars have moved back to our area because they don't want to be bothered to protect them. They don't want to pay the bill.

I click around the TWRA site more. And, hey! One page has a chart of confirmed sightings in Tennessee! It's not a long list, and it hasn't been updated in a while. In fact, the last confirmed sighting was two years before cougars were declared extinct. Hmm . . . that can't be a coincidence, can it? That they stopped updating the list after the state said cougars had totally died off?

But the site gives tips on how to send them information: "What does it take to become an officially confirmed sighting?" it says.

My finger twitches.

This is it. This is my class project.

I push the chair away from my desk, rolling backward, spinning.

If I can confirm my cat is a cougar, I can submit it here and get the state of Tennessee one step closer to protecting her.

I want to get my cougar on that confirmed-sightings list.

I laugh and I think of André and his *Zombie Zoo* comics. My mom and her roadkill. My dad and pretty much all his relationships. Dead and dying things. And me? I'm the opposite.

I want to raise cougars from the dead.

10

PHOENIX. THAT'S YOUR NAME.

Puma, cougar, panther, lion,
Man this project has me cryin'.
This worms through my head while I'm making my backyard rounds that afternoon. Tracking this cougar has me obsessed. So I'm rhyming my way through checking on our "pets," counting carcasses as I rattle off cat names. André would make so much fun of me and these terrible lines. I'm no good at freestyling or slam poetry, but man, do I love them.

While I circle the yard making notes, Ms. Zachary's dogs bark and whine and paw at our chain-link fence. The sound of the fence rattling at our house is near-constant, thanks to those determined dogs.

I barely notice it anymore. The pings and rattles the fence makes are kinda like background music for my lyrics, a soundtrack. Roadkill Radio.

Those dogs aren't getting into our yard, but I admire how unwavering they are in their goal of consuming rotting flesh. Every day they try to dig under the fence (they can't; it's buried a good two feet below ground), or they pace, trying to find a way over it (they *definitely* can't; it's nearly eight feet tall). The smell of this yard punches me in the back of my sinuses every time I walk out here; I can only imagine what their sensitive snoots smell!

Mom's goal is to study roadkill decomposition as close as possible to how it actually occurs in nature— so, an obnoxiously tall fence to keep out the neighbor's dogs. Of course, scraping these animals off pavement and dumping them into our yard is some "scientist intervention" that wouldn't exist otherwise, but overall Mom keeps tight controls on her specimens. And no one else is doing this kind of research, she reminds me often. Our Carcass Farm is one of a kind. Lucky me.

Puma, cougar, panther, lion. Congratulations, Bob Ross! You're the next contestant on Roadkill Roundup!

Subject—Bob Ross: male squirrel (we think—dude was totally road pizza when we gathered him)

Estimated age—4 years

Day—32

Date—November 17

Rainfall—none in the last 24 hours, but soon

Sun exposure—very little—cloudy

Current temperature—34 degrees F

Stage of decomposition—stage 4, advanced decay/butyric
fermentation

Insects present—blowflies, dermestid beetles, carrion
beetles—they're stripping the dried meat off this skeleton
like they're at a beef jerky banquet. We're close to bones
now, baby!

Coloration: green, purplish backside where the body touches
the ground

Odors—strong—gasses cadaverine and putrescine are living
up to their names today! Whew!

Notes—Looks like a carved pumpkin a month after Halloween.
Warped. Hollow. Juices, coloration, smell—all the same as a
weeks-old jack-o'-lantern. Fungi present. CDI: death of all
grass for maybe 6–7 centimeters surrounding

Puma, cougar, panther, lion—you're up, Buttercup!

Subject—Buttercup: female skunk

Estimated age—6 months

Day—3

Date—November 17

Rainfall—none in the last 24 hours, but soon

Sun exposure—very little—cloudy

Current temperature—34 degrees F

Stage of decomposition—stage 1: initial decay/fresh

Insects present—blowflies, maggots. Those flies are laying
more eggs on our Buttercup than the Easter bunny doles
out on Easter.

Coloration: green belly, yellowish skin elsewhere. Fur
beginning to dull. Oily. Sticky.

Odors: I mean, skunk? Also a bit like dry, dusty cheese and
rotting meat.

My stomach growls as I record *cheese* and *meat*. Either I have the healthiest relationship with death ever, or I should seek immediate counseling. Lots to unpack there.

Inside, I hear Mom on the phone. It's obviously Dad she's talking to. Her voice is loud and higher pitched than usual. Squeaky, like she's been sucking air from a birthday balloon. I can only hear one side of the conversation, but hey. Everything feels one-sided with Mom these days.

As soon as I think that, guilt floods me like bile bursting out of a bloated carcass. Nothing else on earth is the color of bile. Nothing else on earth feels as slimy and bile-colored as guilt.

Mom's side of the conversation billows out from our kitchen with the curtains:

"No, David, we've talked about this."

"What's he going to do, travel the country with you, scraping scorpions off the pavement in New Mexico?"

"Okay, Arizona."

"I know that's not all you do." *Heavy sigh.*

"Nope, I'm well aware of the type of research you do. I'm the one doing it *now*, remember?"

"I can't lose that grant money, David. And it—"

"No."

"No, I'm *not* uprooting him from his school."

"This isn't productive. We've had this conversation so many times before. I'm hanging up now, David."

And then, silence.

Ping! I glance at my phone, a welcome distraction. It's a photo of my dad, holding up a dead rattlesnake. He's pinching its jaws so that the mouth is open, fangs protruding. He's posed to look terrified, like the dead snake is attacking him.

This one's for André, ha-ha! it says, with a bunch of dumb emojis after: A snake. A red circle with a line through it. A zombie. Two red exclamation points. A crying-laughing face.

For André? What's for me?

Also, dude gets hung up on and immediately sends a

photo of a rattlesnake to his son? Something about that feels rotten, like he's just, *Oh, well. Another fight with the ex. Time to text the offspring.*

I'm beginning to feel a bit like a weeks-old pumpkin myself. A Jack-o'-lantern. Ha ha.

Thunder rumbles.

The hairs on the back of my neck prickle.

I feel eyes on me.

Yellow eyes.

I turn slowly, toward the back of our yard.

I can't really see her there, the cougar, but I can feel her. I squint and barely make out the graceful curve of her long spine, one massive dangling paw, her huge glowing eyes.

Her eyes. They are magical and terrifying. I imagine her world through them: Scaling tall pine trees. Clinging to jagged mountaintops. Drinking from streams. Padding through snow. Bathing in rain. Sleeping under stars. *Wilderness.*

This is my chance. I slowly raise my phone. Whisper, "Puma, cougar, panther, lion." Snap a picture without looking away. The dogs bark and the fence rattles and the thunder rumbles and my heart pounds.

An icy raindrop hits my skull.

A second one drips on my cheek.

The rain falls quickly.

The screen door bangs. My heart nearly jumps up my esophagus and leaps out of my gaping mouth.

"Jack!" Mom says gleefully. "Rain! Quick—get as many photos as you can!"

On roadkill, one big deluge can do the work of thousands of dermestid beetles, washing bits of muscle and ligament and fur into the soil. Rainfall changes the gasses, the odor, and the bloat of our roadkill. Rain is fast and furious and exciting when you're dead.

I realize I never once looked away from where the cougar was perched, but now she's gone. Disappeared, like something that washes away in the rain.

"Phoenix," I whisper after her. "That's your name. Rising from the dead."

I look at the photo I took with my phone before joining my mom in snapping pics of our waterlogged carcass party. The cat's eyes blend in with the yellow leaves of mid-November, her graceful, curved body looks like a tree branch. Even when I pinch the screen and zoom in, there's not much there.

"Hurry, Jack!" Mom shouts over the cold rainfall. "It's all vanishing so quickly! Hurry!"

11

DISPOSABLE

We're in the swagger wagon, which means it's time to play Roadkill Bingo. And I can tell Mom's in a gathering mood: her eyes shine as they scan the shoulders of the road for anything red and juicy. She keeps muttering stuff like, "more data . . . better numbers . . ." All I want to do is get home from school. Get my weekend started. Play some *Mario Kart*. Scarf some Cheetos.

You might think Mom has some kind of detailed process for finding our new pets, but it's a just matter of using data plus being observant plus luck. (Well, luck if you're us. Unlucky if you're the roadkill.) Mom returns to the roads where she's logged the highest collection of specimens in the past. It might surprise you that these *aren't* major highways; most animals learn to stay away from that noise. And it's not safe for us to pull over and scrape a specimen off the interstate. No, the meatier roads are the busier backroads. Curvy stretches of pavement with lots of trees.

Mom also drives on roads that border creeks and rivers. Animals are thirsty. And in the winter, she looks on roads that the county has salted in case of snow. Deer are drawn to the salt. Other animals are drawn to the deer.

Other animals. They are often the number-one way we find our rabies babies. (Mom hates it when I call them that. These animals rarely have rabies, but I can't resist a tidy rhyme.) So it doesn't surprise me to hear Mom shout, "Buzzards!" She leans over her steering wheel and peers into the gray sky. Carving across the clouds are five or six huge black birds, circling. They never seem to flap their wings, these birds. They just spiral over death endlessly. So creepy.

"Ah, buzzards," Mom chuckles. "My BFFs. Always signaling the way to the good stuff."

Mom turns off the main highway onto a gravel side road, checking the sky, following her BFFs. Best Friends Forever. Buzzards' Funky Food.

We see the heap soon enough. Mom veers the car

over to a wide grassy shoulder and turns on her flashing hazard lights. She grabs orange cones, paint buckets, and the snow shovel from the back. I sigh and follow.

"Look, Jack! It's a pileup!" she sings as she places cones around the site. Sure enough, there are both fur and feathers here. Oh—and scales!

A *pileup* is what Mom calls more than one animal at a site. It happens more than you'd think. As we get closer, I imagine the story playing out: A mouse ran into the road. *Splat!* A snake smelled lunch and followed. *Squish!* A bird saw a two-for-one feast and swooped in for dinner. *Squawk!*

Mom bends over, plucks a soggy brown apple core out of the ditch on the opposite side of the road. She *tsks*. Sighs. Shakes her head. "Somebody threw this apple core out their window and it killed three animals."

Why did the mouse cross the road? To get to the litter on the other side. But plot twist: *Splat!* I swallow hard.

Mom is talking into her voice recorder: "Buck Hollow Road. Eastern deer mouse. Snake—looks like a garter. Turkey buzzard. Postmortem interval . . ." She pauses here and toes each animal. They're cold and stiff, and they turn as if they've been taxidermized. "Maybe five hours? But it's cold today, below freezing, so perhaps four."

I head for the mouse first. Here's the thing about gravel roads: they're awesome. Just dig underneath and heft the specimen into the bucket. Easy-peasy. Much better than trying to scrape entrails off hot tar.

For this mouse's roadside memorial, I place a small, smooth rock where the mouse expired. It blends in with the rest of the gravel, but I know it's there. And I figure it's pretty mouse-like, that rock; present but not really seen.

There aren't a lot of cars whizzing by, so Mom's hunched over the snake rather than waving traffic around the site. When I approach with a second bucket, Mom points to a long, cylindrical pellet, swirled with black and brown and white. "Our snake here literally got the poop knocked out of him!"

She says it with too much joy. I huff in the cold air and scoop. Up and in you go, Nagini. The snake is memorialized with a smooth, slender stick.

It reminds me of the photo of my dad and the rattle-snake.

My dad. He's the one who started the roadside memorials. Markers like the crosses you sometimes see on the side of the highway, white ones covered in plastic flowers. "It's just too much sometimes, bud," he said once, gently lifting a gem-colored bluebird into a bucket. He fished in his pocket and drew out a jackknife. He cut a blue button off his flannel shirt and placed it where she had lain. "These animals are just doing their thing, following their instincts, and we humans plow through our lives not even *seeing* them, you know? These animals aren't disposable."

I've been thinking about that a lot lately, *disposable*. Animals. People. It's too easy to plow right through our lives and not see things for what they are. I worry sometimes that Mom loses sight of things or thinks of them as just specimens. Experiments. Disposable.

Dad always *felt* more than Mom, and I think these memorials were his way of coping with all this gore. Of seeing them as animals and not just specimens. Of ushering them into the Big After. I don't like to think about that too much, the After.

Anyway, these roadside memorials? They help.

"And this poor fella's got a bit of road rash," Mom says of the buzzard. Feathers are everywhere, and his skin shows bumpy, red, raw underneath. He's bucketed and sealed and stored. I place a slick magnolia leaf where the bird was. The shiny leaf reminds me of a sleek bird feather.

"Let's head home," I say. "I've got homework." Mom's picking up the cones, but she's not listening. Her eyes are still skyward. I feel a lump of dread in my stomach as I follow her gaze up to the clouds.

The buzzards are still circling.

"There's *more!*" Mom shouts. "Huzzah for the Vulture Culture!" She jangles her keys and hops in the driver's seat. "What a day!"

"What a day," I echo.

ENDANGERED? EXTINCT?

We see it quickly: a deer. Smallish, but healthy. She'd easily fit in the hatch of our swagger wagon.

"There's no way she'll fit in our swagger wagon," I say.

Mom *pshaws* me. She's already slammed the car in park and is grabbing the orange cones.

She pulls on long blue rubber gloves. "Ah, she's a beauty! Intact, no external fluids to worry about. Grab your gloves, Jack! She's going in!"

I huff loudly to make my displeasure known. But I pull on my gloves and join her.

When we try to lift her (a small deer still weighs about forty pounds), it's clear that this deer has been in rigor mortis for a while. We try cramming her into the back of the wagon, but her legs are so stiff she won't budge.

"Let's leave her here, Mom." I hear a bit of whine in my voice. "We have two deer already!"

But Mom's face has changed. Instead of the joyful person who already found three specimens today, her face has hardened. Anger. Rigor mortis.

"No. This deer is intact and she's coming home with me."

She's like a hoarder, but for roadkill.

And then? Mom starts massaging the dead deer. Kneading the joints and flanks. The muscles snap and pop, the sound of someone cracking their knuckles. It's a process called breaking rigor, and it sounds like snapping bones, but it's just loosening the stiff, dead muscles. It sounds *awful*. My stomach flops.

There's a soft daytime moon hanging in the sky. A daytime moon always feels so sci-fi; it reminds me that here we are, crawling across a planet rolling through space.

There's no life on that soft, dry moon. No creatures at all. No bacteria or bugs or beetles or buzzards of any kind. It must be so quiet. So clean.

"Mom . . ."

POP!

Mom loosens one of the doe's legs enough to bend it beneath her. "There!" she says, stepping back and dusting her hands. "Now you'll fit! C'mon, Jack!"

Mom's face has changed again and is now content but determined. Stage Two Decomposition, after rigor breaks and bloat begins.

We get the doe loaded in the back of our station wagon, and Mom slams the hatch shut with a smile. She wipes her sweaty brow with the back of her gloved hand. "Whew. She's a healthy one."

"Is she?" I mutter. I eye Mom, but my hint at *her* health is lost in her excitement. I climb inside the passenger seat of our roadkill hearse.

We're about halfway home before I realize: I forgot to put out a marker for this deer.

We drag the doe to the middle of the yard. I don't want to admit that she *is* a nice specimen. No external bleeding, all her parts—face, hooves, body—intact. She'll be great research. I name her Belle.

When Belle has her resting spot in our Roadkill Garden, I look at Mom. I have to peer through my too-long bangs, and I try tucking them aside. Mom smiles at me but doesn't seem to notice. Doesn't she see the life that keeps going on out *here*? Hair that keeps growing and nails that need trimming and *feelings*?

Me and Mom—endangered? Extinct? What is the cost *there*?

I fall asleep that night thinking about what I could've put on the gravel road to memorialize Belle. A crisp brown leaf, likely. The sound of Ms. Zachary's dogs rattling our chain-link fence lulls me to sleep.

SCIENTIST OR SURGEON OR BUTCHER

"Jack! Get out here! You gotta come see this!"

Mom yelling from the backyard wakes me up. It's a blue-sky day but cold, deeply cold. I rub sleep from my eyes, kick on some Crocs, and head outside.

I am *not* prepared for what I see next.

First, there is not a turkey buzzard to be seen. Odd.

But also? Belle, our perfect specimen of a doe, has been dragged to the far corner of the yard, near the woodpile. The dragging of this forty-pound doe across our yard took out three other roped-off research pods.

Mom is standing over the deer carcass. The deer has been shaved (*shaved?!*) and sliced with a single, precise cut. Like one made by a scientist. Or a surgeon. Or a butcher.

And, well. Organs are missing.

But it's all so . . . clean? I'm not used to seeing clean entrails. I shiver.

In art class, we've been studying famous artists. One of the artists—his name is Jackson Pollock—stands above his canvas and flings gobs of paint down on it. *Splat, sling*—a splatter painting. That's the kind of entrails I'm used to seeing with our roadkill. Messy and bright.

But this other artist, his name is Kandinsky. This guy paints with rulers and compasses—perfect, precise lines; full, round circles. Geometry and balance.

That's what this deer looks like. Dissected. Disassembled.

It's easier to put aside *this was an alive animal* with splatter.

Mom and I stand over the deer, speechless. At last, Mom whispers, "Didn't you say you saw a cougar?"

My heart leaps into my throat and I'm shaking my head before my voice starts working. Up to this point, I thought maybe I had been dreaming it. You know—stress or magic or something. An imaginary friend. "I don't . . . I can't be sure it was a cougar."

"I think we can be sure now."

We both stand there, creeped out, as our breath disappears into blue. Is the cougar watching us now, as we examine her handiwork? I shiver again.

Mom swallows, nods. "And I'm no cougar expert, but this . . . this isn't normal behavior. Stalking animals that are already dead. That cat is under duress."

I haven't done a whole lot of my project yet—I mean, it's not due for another ten days—but from what I've read, she's right. Cougars hunt live deer, they don't prey on dead ones. A cougar would have to be very sick or very hungry to do something like this.

"We can't have this." Mom bites her lip and paces. "That cougar can't be here. We definitely have to run her off." Her brow wrinkles and she stares into the trees lining the back of our property, like she's waiting for this cougar to march out here and explain herself. "This is going to skew all my data," she mutters. "Going to throw all the grant numbers into a tailspin . . ."

I blink hard at the mention of our grant. Anything that throws off Mom's research could—*splat!*—kill off our funding like a bug on a windshield.

"I heard the fence rattling last night, but I thought it was the dogs," I say without thinking. Did this happen because I didn't put a marker down on the road for this doe, memorialize her in some small way? Did she become disposable? Nah, surely the universe doesn't work like that.

Mom's pacing is making me nervous. She's now looking from the fence to the three ruined research plots. "This isn't good. This . . . isn't good. The data is due at the end of the year, Jack. That's just a few weeks away. We can't have this cat eating our data! We could lose our funding. That grant money—*oh, mercy*."

I agree. A cougar leaping over our eight-foot fence and eating the things that pay our bills is not good. But my priority right now is making sure Mom doesn't make a rash decision. Doesn't fall into one of her dark moods. I know what Dad would do.

"Too bad this cougar isn't into Vivaldi instead of vermin," I say with a nervous chuckle. A composer versus decomposer joke. And not a very good one.

But Mom blinks two or three times, then a slow smile spreads across her face. She laughs.

"Okay, yes. This might add a fascinating new element to the data. Think positive, Jennifer," she tells herself. "But it has to be temporary. This cougar *cannot stay*." Mom whips out her voice recorder and lists the details of the crime scene. I almost feel like we should chalk off the body. I walk the fence line, feeling a thrill of excitement and nausea.

A hunch leads me to the woodpile, and I glance up. There, tangled in the very tip-top of our fence, is a sandy tuft of fur.

I look back at Mom, but she's moved on to taking

photos of Belle with her phone. I slowly scale the log pile and reach up to try and grab the fur. It's too high.

I take a photo of the fur, and when I zoom in, I can see that the strands are tipped with black. I pocket my phone and try again to reach it, but nope.

A stick. I rumble around in the log pile and pull out a stick. If I can jimmy the tuft of fur loose . . .

The moment the stick touches the fur, the tuft floats off on the wind, like a dandelion seed. Can I make a wish on a floating furball? *Come back, tiny fluff!*

I watch the fur drift and curl, then land like a feather in a pile of leaves. I can swing around the fence and get that.

But Mom is done taking notes and photos, and she's resumed the pacing and the lip-biting. "Okay, so this is a fascinating anomaly. A cool blip in the data. But this cat, she can't make this a habit. This can't be one of her regular grazing spots. It's too dangerous for her to be here. *She's* dangerous."

I glance down at Belle the deer. Her soft body is splayed open, her organs sliced away, stolen.

I shiver. She's right. What am I *doing,* trying to save an animal like Phoenix? What kind of creature is this cougar? Was I fooled? Duped? *Why* am I such a terrible judge of character? Why do I believe in people who always seem to let me down?

But something gnaws at the back of my brain like a

busy dermestid beetle. This cat—she's *nature*, just like the bugs and buzzards and mushrooms that overtake our roadkill. She's just in the wrong place. She and her cousin cats wandered all the way here, from a long way away. And this one's wandered too far. There is a better home for her than here.

But I have to prove she even exists before we can help her. She's good at being overlooked. An expert in being ignored.

Cat, you and I have a lot in common.

Can I change my wish on that drifting furball? I wish again for a trail camera.

Mom cracks her knuckles, determined. "We have to run this cat off. Sooner, rather than later."

She marches into the house, apparently headed to research *how to chase off a cougar.*

I sigh. Proving a cougar exists has been hard enough without actively driving it away.

I plop down on one of the logs in the pile and look at the photo of the fur again. I have to step up my efforts to find this cat. Mom is pretty much an expert at driving things away.

Ugh! I feel bad as soon as I think it. I know she's doing her best. And hey—she's the parent who's still *here.*

Guilt feels like the beginning stages of putrefaction—green and bloated.

HER SIDE OF THE FENCE

André arrives about an hour later, and he's as happy as a maggot in an eye socket when he sees that the vultures are currently MIA. When I show him why, though, he gulps.

"Dude," he whispers. He peeks at Belle out of the corner of his eye, his grossed-out face tucked into his shoulder. "That is *sick*."

I nod. "We have to go behind the fence."

"No. No, we don't."

"Her fur is back there. I need it for my project."

André is shaking his head, but he says, "I need a baseball bat. Or a rake. Or a samurai sword."

I smile. *That's* why André's the best.

We clang out of the front gate, walk past Ms.

Zachary's barking dogs, and turn left around the back fence line. The grass is overgrown here, and the leaves pile high on the ground, wet and moldy. The sun melts through tree branches and filters through the leaves that haven't yet made the leap to earth. I breathe in deep; it smells like fall.

André is hunched low, and he clutches the golf club he selected as his weapon. His eyes scan the forest. "This feels *exactly* like those moments when you scream at the horror movie, 'Don't go into the *woods*! Are you crazy?'"

I laugh, but he's not wrong.

I have my camera in one hand and a rake in the other. This old camera is awkward—it's chunky and it has no strap—and I have to keep shuffling it from hand to hand to balance both tools. I put the camera down and use the rake to poke around the spot where I thought the tuft of fur fell. Nothing's here. It flew away, melted into the soft sun. Am I *sure* this cougar is real?

I look back at our house. Belle is pushed up against the chain-link fence, her fur poking through in diamond patterns, like the cat thought maybe she could shove this deer through to the other side. To *her* side of the fence.

Where we are now. Her side. My heart races, thinking about that.

She's real, all right.

I flip over a mushy log with my rake and watch dozens of bugs scurry for cover. I poke through tall crunchy brown grass. I kick a mushroom. And then I see it.

Scat.

Cat poo. It is big (gross) and round (weird) and firm (ugh) when I push it with my rake. "André, check it out."

His eyes flick down at the scat. "Mmm-hmm. We ready to go?"

"One more minute."

I snap a few photos before I cut it apart with my rake. It's dry and not as easy to slice as I expected. And, oh! Inside the scat are tufts of gray fur and tiny bones. Mouse leftovers.

"Dude, look!"

André blinks at the scat and lowers his club at last. "Wow!" He whips out his sketch book and starts scratching pencil over paper. I take more photographs. *Click! Click!*

"Let's head back," I say after taking fifty or sixty more poo photos.

André nods, grabs his club, and sprints back around the fence.

When we get to the yard, the vultures are starting to return. The cougar must be far away currently. André scowls at the birds but starts sketching a squished skunk. The skunk's front right paw is raised high and stiff in the air, like he wants to ask a question in class.

"Seriously, your mom's job is the coolest. But these guys," André waves his pencil point in the direction of the vultures, "they're the worst job perk ever."

I'm not listening too closely, because I'm scanning through the photos on the camera's tiny screen.

"They're not so bad," I say, not looking up from my poo photography. I've captured the *essence* of scat in these, if I do say so myself. The turd practically glistens. "You should see what some of the folks in Mom's department have to deal with."

André looks up from his sketch. "Like what?"

I resume flipping through my on-screen art. "Well, I mean, this one guy at the university. He does all sorts of things with roadkill. He buries them and digs them up again. He turns them into compost. He covers them with yogurt or chemicals. He dries them in the sun. He soaks them in jars of water. He boils them. He microwaves them."

I look up at last, and André is fully green, pencil hovering over paper, staring at me, mouth wide. Stage Two Decomposition: bloat and discoloration. I laugh.

"Can you imagine eating popcorn out of *that* microwave?"

André shakes his head fast, like he's fighting bile.

He slams his sketchbook and pencil into his backpack. "Nope. Nope. I don't believe you this time. Nope."

I shrug. "Wouldn't be the first time someone didn't believe me."

"Nope," André mutters. He hops on his bike and clicks the strap on his helmet.

"Don't forget—I need your help picking my *Zombie Zoo* strips," he says.

I inhale. "I know. I will."

André takes one more look at our Roadkill Garden and pedals away. "NOPE!" he shouts over his shoulder back at me.

I laugh again.

I'm used to people not believing me when I tell them what my mom's job is. I'm used to people not believing me when I say we don't eat the roadkill we collect. I'm used to people not believing me when I tell them I'm not morbid or obsessed with death or some weirdo who likes collecting dead things.

And it doesn't make a difference whether they believe those things or not.

I push a button on my camera, and up comes another glistening photo of scat.

But *this*? I want people to believe *this*—that this cougar is here, in Tennessee, in *my backyard*. It's the truth, and I want people to know.

I need people to believe me on this.

Because this cougar: she's mysterious and strong and she fends for herself. Totally self-reliant, all while invisible. Stealthy. *Until* she needs help. "Under duress," Mom called it. And now that she's hurting, hungry, she's letting us know. My teachers all say, "Advocate for yourself." That's what this cougar is doing. I admire that.

I can do the invisible part just great. I want to learn how to do the other part. I want to learn how to say, *Hey, little help over here?*

Other people, they can't help a hurt if they don't even know it's there. You can't heal silent sadness.

I need to prove she's here so I can help her.

I need to know that speaking up for yourself actually works.

IT'S US OR THEM

Ms. Bennett said we have to use at least three sources for our report that aren't off the internet. Books, magazine articles, newspaper pieces . . . things you can't find and read through Google. So that afternoon, I blow off my work, dust off my bike, and take off to the library.

The library. I haven't been here in . . . who knows how long. Our city's library is newish, with glass doors that slide open like a grocery store. The smell of books welcomes me, and I smile. When I walk in, the librarian looks at me like she knows me, but can't think of my name. And that's okay—she can't remember *all* her customers, right?

But she smiles. "Ah, so good to see you again! Are you here with your dad?"

Hmmph. That's how long it's been since I've been to the library.

The library is Dad's territory. Not that Mom hates the library—I mean, who hates a library?—but she's not a regular here. Dad, he was a regular. Poetry, non-fiction, true crime, thrillers—he read all of it. Wanted to discuss all of it. Made friends with librarians and went to author events because of all of it.

I wonder if he's found a library near his new apartment. I wonder if he's visiting a library while he's in Arizona. I wouldn't know.

I ignore the librarian's question. "Can you point me to information on cougars?"

"Absolutely!" She beams. She wheels out from behind the desk, and I follow her to the nonfiction section in the kids' department. The back of her wheelchair has stickers of Pokémon, a peace sign, a rainbow flag, and a bumper sticker that says "No Hitchhikers."

"Section 599.74. Enjoy!" she says. She leaves me in the aisle. It's quiet and the shelves are colorful. I stand there and grin for a minute. If I had to pick a place that was the opposite of a dirty, smelly, loud roadside, this would likely be it.

I flip through books with straightforward titles like

Cougars and *Mountain Lions* and *Pumas* and *Panthers*. The slick photos are cool, but the information is all basic. What they eat, where they live—that kind of thing. I take notes, but I wonder if there are any cougar books for adults? Stuff with, you know . . . more *meat*.

The themes I keep finding over and over: Cougars are dangerous. Cougars should be avoided. Cougars and humans cannot live in harmony. Cougars should be chased away.

Bright-yellow-caution-tape-type information. My mom would fully agree.

I'm feeling a lot of doubt about this project. Why do I want to protect something so dangerous? Why am I so drawn to this big cat?

And then I stumble across a poem in one of the books. Poetry, of course. The poem is called "Mountain Lion" by D. H. Lawrence. One line says this: "And I think in this empty world there was room for me and a mountain lion."

There is room for us both. All those other books, they were making it sound like it's us or them. But we can coexist. We *do*. It's a simple truth, but it is true. Poetry is like that. That's why it's so cool, why I like it so much. Poetry says things that are so obvious it takes your breath away. Like a punch, but with words. I wish I could write it.

Poetry and photography both do that. They freeze a moment and make it special.

I found my answer—*I want to find room for us both*. Dad would love that poetry did that, gave me the answer. He'd be so excited he'd help me search for every cougar poem ever written.

Suddenly my heart twists like it's being yanked from my chest cavity by a hungry turkey buzzard. I blinkblinkblink because my eyes sting. *No crying in the library!* I tell myself.

I miss my dad.

In our house, there's *not* enough room for both him and Mom. So Dad was chased away. Mom chases away the things that I want to stay. And I guess I'm on team *us* because I haven't been invited to team *them*.

When I get home, Mom squints at me from across the backyard. "Where have you been?" she shouts. She's not angry, really, but she's loud.

"The library. I texted you," I answer.

She waves that off like texts are nothing but pesky flies. "I need to know when you won't be doing the logs."

"I texted you," I repeat. "And it's for school."

"Tell me next time," she says, and she huffs her bangs off her forehead. "So I know when I need to do

79

them." She turns back to Freddy, our newest rabbit, and starts typing on the tablet.

I pinch my lips. "A text *is* telling you," I mutter. The screen door bangs loudly behind me as I go inside, and I don't do anything to soften its slam.

ALBERT EINSTEIN'S DYING WORDS

Made another *Zombie Zoo* comic last night. Check it out."

The next morning, André and I are bouncing along on our green plastic bus seat. André hands over his sketchbook. The first panel shows what is obviously scat, brand-new and steaming, with a tangle of fur and bones woven inside. I smile. He was inspired by our find a couple days ago.

Second panel: the turd starts to twitch.

Panel three: the bones rise slowly from the steaming poo. By panel four, they've assembled themselves into a frail mouse skeleton. He even places a tiny mouse beret on his tiny mouse skull. "BRAIIIINNNSSSS!" he moans.

In panel five, the zombie mouse's nose twitches. In the next series of panels, he looks around, sees where he is standing.

"Why do I smell like this?" Zombie Mouse asks. "Have I been . . . swallowed? Digested? Am I . . . I am . . . *poo*?!" The zombie mouse is scooping up handfuls of the scat in which he still stands.

"Mon dieu!" Zombie Mouse cries, and the bones collapse back into the poo. He's died again.

I laugh. "Mon dieu?"

André smiles smugly. "It's French. Apparently, they're the most-often-said dying words."

"Huh," I say. I trace my fingers over the speech bubble. The words sound like poetry, like a short prayer. "You know, when Albert Einstein died, he uttered something that was likely brilliant, right? But nobody knows what his dying words were. He was in an American hospital, and he spoke his last words in German."

It's the kind of fact I wish I didn't know but somehow I do. Likely Dad told me that.

"Is that right?" André says. He pauses, and the bus hits a pothole. We fly a solid six inches off our seat. The whole bus creaks and moans.

"Do you know what your dying words will be?" André asks.

Why do people always ask me stuff like this? "Uh, *no*." I say, a bit too defensively. "Morbid much?"

André grins. "I know mine. I'm going to be lying there, all dry and thirsty, and I'm going to croak out, 'The treasure is buried—' *KKKKKCHHHHT*." He closes his eyes, cocks his head, sticks out his tongue. His impression of instant death. I don't have the heart to tell him that instant death looks more wide-eyed and fluid-filled. More "Mon dieu!" But I laugh.

"Cliffhanger death. Nice."

"Kinda like old Albert."

"Yeah."

André drums on the top of the seat in front of us until the girl in that seat, Beatrice, turns and scowls at him. He shrugs and stops. "Hey, Jack. When, uh . . . when do you think you can help me pick those samples for the contest? I really need to—"

"Can't today," I interrupt. I don't know why, but his twitchiness is suddenly getting on my nerves. André never gets on my nerves. "Gotta work."

"I could come by your house this afternoon. I don't think it'll take long. I just need to pick five . . ."

I'm already shaking my head. He doesn't *get it*. I have a job now. I can't just read cartoons all day.

"Nope. Too much work to do."

I hear how snappy I sound, and I get angry at myself.

André purses his lips. "Whatever." He looks out the window the rest of the ride.

Mon dieu.

When I get off the bus, I'm still angry at André for *not getting it*, and angry at myself for being such a goober to him about it. All that irritation must've temporarily blinded me or something, because while I'm watching the tips of my Converse enter the school, I run smack into—

"Zoe!" I say. "I'm, uh, sorry!"

It's just like the movies, except neither of us does that thing where paper and books fly everywhere, and we have *a moment* while scooping them up. Nope. It was just two people crashing into each other, and it kind of hurt.

Zoe rubs her arm where I ran into her. "Jack?" she says. She blinks, and her confusion melts into a smile.

"I'm sorry," I say. "Are you okay?"

"Sure," she says. "Listen, I've been meaning to ask you . . ."

She pauses there, and I wonder if crashing into her has changed her mind about whatever it is she wants to ask me. Ask *me*. "Yeah?"

She shifts on her feet, works her jaw. Then, it all

spills out, like intestinal fluid on impact.

"Your mom. She's an environmental scientist, right? I mean, I think she is? And I head up the environmental club—" here, she vaguely gestures at her T-shirt. Today it reads *Support Your Local Planet.* "And so I thought she might be a great speaker. She could come in, tell us about her job . . ."

Ah, so that's it. That's why she's been so nice to me lately. Zoe wants to be my friend so she can learn more about my weird family, my morbid mom.

Anger burbles up again. I'd rather stand in the middle of the main school hallway in the Hulk underwear I wore in kindergarten than have my mom here, at my school, talking to Zoe about roadkill.

"She's, uh, really busy," I say. I have get out of here, *now.* But I don't want to tell her no for some reason. She just seems so . . . genuinely interested. "Bye!"

"Bye," Zoe says behind me. "Maybe later?"

I hear her, kind of, but I tune it out. I will just keep tuning it all out.

"WHAT'S NEXT, DAD?"

Go ahead and get started without me," Mom yells from inside the house. "We'll get a little log work done before Odette arrives."

Sure, yeah, okay. *I'll just do your work for you.* I immediately feel gross for thinking it, as cold and hollow as Stage One Decomposition.

The tablet screen wakes up with a tap of my finger. I bet we're the only household in America that has a photo of a squished squirrel as their wallpaper, his dull tail sticking up from the pavement as straight and fuzzy as a toilet brush.

A chill chases down my spine, almost like the feeling you get when the sun ducks behind clouds. Movement. In the trees.

I'm drawn to it like a blowfly to strewn intestines. I put the tablet on top of our rusty grill and circle around behind the fence.

The woods today are the kind of magic you only see in late fall: the sun and the shadows playing tag, the leaves dancing toward the ground, the limbs yawning and stretching and preparing for their big sleep. The trees groan and the wind sings and the earth smells like a musky, smoky hug—someone down the road a bit must be burning leaves.

A stick cracks.

"Hey. What're we looking for?"

I spin, but I don't see him. Dad. It's his voice.

"Dad?"

"What're we looking for?"

Okay, I'm officially losing it. But I play along, because there has to be *some* reason I'm imagining my dad's voice. "A cougar."

"*Ahhhh, I saw a cougar once.*" His voice echoes through my head. I turn, but there are only rays of silent sunlight beaming through the leaves.

"Yeah?"

"*Yeah. Scared me so much I puma pants.*" Dad laughs at his own joke. At *my* joke, that my brain assigned to him.

I shake my head. Imagining Dad jokes? I'm worse off than I thought.

I breathe in deeply. Spin slowly. No Phoenix. No Dad.

"*I miss these adventures of ours, bud,*" Dad says.

"Me too. But you left, Dad. You ended these adventures. You ran away."

Imaginary Dad has nothing to say to that.

"I miss talking to you, Dad." *Obviously*, I think. Why else would I be out here talking to a bunch of tree trunks? "You always understood things, like why Zoe makes my stomach flop and when I do dumb stuff like snap at André. I can't talk as much with Mom. And it's worse now. She's . . . different. She doesn't even want to do Legos anymore. That kit—it's been on our dining room table for weeks."

Not-Dad sighs. "*She's sad, Jack. A divorce. It's like a death.*" I turn and blink through the bright sun, looking into our backyard at our roadkill graveyard. Bones and fur and teeth and patches of brown grass.

A death? So . . . is there a Big After in divorce? What does that look like? What kind of memorial do you place at the end of a marriage? What kind of words do you say then?

"What's next, Dad?"

"Dad?"

Dad?

A yellow leaf falls. I extend my hand, but it's just past my reach.

Dad's gone. Ran away again. And I still have all these questions and no answers. Just *once* I'd like for an adult—even a pretend adult!—to simply say *I don't know*. It's so much better than being ignored.

THE BONE ZONE

Mom checks her watch. "Odette should be here any minute." Her eyes flick to the corner of the yard. True to her researcher nature, she hasn't moved Belle. But our cougar doesn't seem to have returned. Mom wanders closer, scanning the trees.

She squats over the doe. She snaps on bright blue plastic gloves and gently, gently folds back Belle's fur with a pair of tweezers from her pocket. Mom always has a pair of tweezers in her pocket. Lots of ticks in this line of work.

"Fascinating," she says for the thousandth time, looking into the doe's chest cavity. "It almost looks like the muscles have been scraped away with sandpaper, doesn't it? That's one powerful cat tongue."

Mom bites her lip, looks up into the trees again from her squat. "We need some lights back here. Maybe a sound cannon. That would chase our unwelcome visitor away."

An oddly protective feeling washes over me. For the cat. Mom was right about this cougar being "under duress." I've done some more research, and this cat wouldn't normally mess with carrion. She's hungry.

"You know, Mom," I say, bouncing on my toes. "We're getting a little low in inventory lately, don't you think?" I sweep my arm across our backyard, dotted with dying patches of grass and carcasses.

Mom stands slowly, snapping off her gloves and giving me the side-eye. This is very different from my usual stance on all this, which is *no way do we need* another *stinking carcass*. She can see right through me; surely she knows I just want to feed Phoenix.

But Mom's face shifts into a slow smile. "Bud, thank you for that enthusiasm! Yes! After Odette gets here, let's go hunting!"

She gives me a quick side-hug, and I feel both guilty and pleased. Bloating plus putrefaction. But if Phoenix needs more to eat, I want to help. If she's asking for help, I want to offer it.

"Knock-knock," Odette yells, banging the chain-link

gate open and closed. "The bone collector's here!"

Mom laughs. I join her, because Odette is wearing head-to-toe iridescent green—the kind of shiny material that looks purply in some light, golden in others. And I do mean head to toe—she's sporting an iridescent green top hat, tuxedo jacket, pants, and boots. And with her thick, round glasses, she looks like a June bug.

Odette's large, round blinky eyes scan the backyard. "Where's David?"

Mom's jaw shifts slightly. "He, uh . . . We're separated. Different views of the world and whatnot."

Different views of the world? Don't we all have different views of the world? How can that possibly be a reason for a divorce? My lips pinch together.

Odette shifts on her platform boots. "Oh, I didn't know. I'm sorry."

I feel them both not looking at me. Like, not looking at me *really hard*.

It's quiet then. Uncomfortable quiet. There's all these unsaid words hanging in the air, and if I weren't here, they'd say them. This is one of those moments where these two have the chance, right now, to become closer friends. But they don't say anything, they don't do it, because I'm here.

I'm here.

Odette clears her throat. "Whatcha got for me, Jennifer?" Odette can't be thirty years old, but she somehow feels like a grandma. Maybe it's the job. *Skeleton articulator* feels like a job only an ancient, dusty person would have.

Mom's eyes light up. "Some real beauts. I've got an armadillo right over here . . ."

Mom leads Odette to the armadillo first. King Arthur, I call him. All that armor. Odette squats. She circles. She toes the bones gently. She snaps dozens of photos.

"Hmmph," she declares at last. "Shell's cracked. Couple bits missing."

My mom raises an eyebrow. "Easy fixes for an artist like you, Odette."

Odette scowls.

Mom points out the undercarriage of the armadillo. Most folks don't know, but an armadillo's belly is fluffy and furry and soft. When they're alive and not fully decomposed, that is.

"Not a hair follicle in sight, Odette. Not a flake of skin. My necrophages should be called Mr. Clean, they're so good at scrubbing up bones."

By *scrubbing* she means *eating* and by *necrophages* she means *organisms that devour dead things*.

"I'll give you fifty dollars for her."

"Odette, I know you'll charge three hundred for her on Odette's Oddities. Let's say seventy-five."

Odette grins. "I haven't told you my new Etsy shop name? It's now the Bone Zone."

"The Bone Zone—catchy!" Mom says.

"Easier for people to find me that way," Odette says, scowling at the armadillo. "Seventy dollars."

Mom shoots me a quick wink. I feel a swirl of pride at her negotiating skills, like buzzing flies around a fresh corpse.

"What else?" Odette asks, scanning our Roadkill Garden.

"Ah, wait'll you see!" Mom leads Odette over to a curled skeleton, fully intact. "A cottonmouth snake!" Kaa, I called her. Like the snake from *The Jungle Book*.

A look of *holy cow what beautiful bones* flashes across Odette's face. I wish I didn't know what that expression looks like, but I do.

Odette doesn't even circle or touch the snake. "One hundred dollars."

"One fifty," Mom counters.

"I can't do one fifty, Jennifer," Odette says.

Mom shrugs. "My dermestids sure did a nice clean-up job on this one." She points, her finger swirling in the air, following the curl of the snake. "Not a bone missing. Not a joint out of socket."

"One twenty-five."

Mom sighs. "I'm afraid I need one fifty. I guess I could call Bob . . ."

Odette stiffens at the name of her biggest competitor, Bob Jones of Bob Jones's Bones. She shoves her thick glasses up the bridge of her nose. "I'll take it."

We leave Odette to pick apart the bones in our yard with *her* tweezers, labeling each vertebra with a soft, faint pencil. She will reassemble them at her studio like a delicate jigsaw puzzle and sell them online for three times what she's paid us for them. People pay a lot for snake vertebrae, posed to look real.

"Ready to scrape?" Mom says with glee. She dangles her keys.

No, is my automatic reply. I'm still frustrated about the whole *different views of the world* thing. This is the first I've heard of that.

But Phoenix is hungry.

I fake a smile. I feel like my teeth look like a row of snake vertebrae, posed to look real. Surely Mom senses this—that this behavior of mine is as odd and unusual as a cougar going after roadkill. But she doesn't see it, of course. When your relationship is endangered, borderline extinct, you overlook a lot.

I grin wider. "Let's scrape."

JACK SPLAT

Ping!

A text from Dad:

Fun fact: a "retort" is not only a snappy reply to someone's argument—it's also the name of the big machine where cremations happen. Big fire. Bone dust. All that. So when someone says, "Nice *retort*, dude," they're saying, "Sick burn!" HA! Miss you, bud. Love you. Take care of your Mom.

It's followed by a bunch of fire emojis and a couple skeleton ones. Why does Dad love emojis so much? *Gah*—so dumb.

Also? Who says, "Nice retort, dude"?!

"Your phone, Mr. Acosta?" Ms. Bennett says, peering over her cat-eye glasses at me. "You know the rules.

You use it, you lose it." She flips her hand in that *bring it here* motion. I sigh and take it to her at the front of the class.

"Ooooh, Jack Splat got busted," Cameron loud-whispers. A couple of kids nearby crackle with laughter.

"Shut up," I mutter.

Nice retort, dude.

Also also? Who texts their kid something like that when they know their kid is in class? Well, *should* know their kid is in class. Ms. Bennett tucks my phone in a desk drawer.

"Okay, Earthlings!" Ms. Bennett singsongs. "We're six days away from presenting our projects! So. I'd like a one-paragraph essay from each of you on where your project currently stands. Just a quick summary of the things you've found out already."

The class collectively groans. Cameron is by far the loudest, tossing his head back and rolling his eyes, acting like writing words on paper is torture.

But it is, I soon find. I *taptaptap* the tip of my pencil against the blank sheet of paper. All I have are photos of some fur, a paw print, and some scat. A handful of basic facts from some easy reader books. Oh, and a mauled deer.

I'm going to fail. I'm going to get an F on this project

and fail Earth Science. Science—the one subject that should run in my DNA. Both Mom *and* Dad's jam. Of all the courses to fail . . . I'm going to further cement my standing as the Roadkill Kid—Project DOA. (Or, in roadkill terms, DOR: "Dead on Road.")

"Okay, pass your papers up," Ms. Bennett says.

I look down at my paper. It's covered in tiny dots, like the fleas that jump off a dead animal the moment the carcass starts cooling. I ball up the piece of paper.

I don't turn anything in.

I've never *not turned anything in.*

When the bell finally rings, I slam my notebook shut. Jam it into my backpack. Dash up to Ms. Bennett's desk.

She's flipping my phone over and over in the palm of her hand. She peers at me like I'm a specimen to be studied.

"Uh, my phone?" I ask, shifting my weight from foot to foot. "Can I—"

"Do you have a minute, Mr. Acosta?"

Without thinking, my eyes dart to the hallway. Zoe and Cameron are both just outside the door.

"N-not really?" I stammer. "Lunch . . ."

Ms. Bennett looks to where I've glanced toward the hall and nods. She knows we get, like, eight minutes for lunch.

"Maybe later?" I say, and cringe, because *why* offer to come back?

"Later," Ms. Bennett says. She offers me my phone. I leave.

Cameron is still right outside the door. Lockers bang and kids bump and backpacks jostle and is it really hot out here?

"Jack Splat . . ." Cameron repeats. A couple of his buddies guffaw.

And here's the thing. It is funny. But that's all he says. Doesn't even follow it up with something meaty, something like, *So you're going to repeat seventh grade because you're failing science, huh?*

I smash my lips together, but it doesn't stop what I say next.

"Intelligence can't live in a vacuum," I say.

"What?" Cameron smirks.

"Exactly."

From behind me comes the sound of laughter, bold like wind chimes. I turn and there she is.

Zoe's eyes are crinkled and her freckles are dancing, and I feel like my belly is full of the bacteria that eats your organs after you pass.

She smacks my arm lightly with the back of her hand. "Dude. I was *not* ready for that essay today."

"Me neither," Cameron says. He smiles at her.

My voice is stolen by organ-eating bacteria, I believe.

"Anyway, want to come over and work on our projects tomorrow? I could use the motivation."

I swallow. My esophagus still works, thankfully. Cameron and his buddies are watching me, waiting for me to hit Stage Three Decomposition: Active Decay. Loss of fluid through bodily orifices.

I nod. "Uh, sure."

"Great! Give me your phone."

Somehow, I find my phone in my jacket pocket. She types her number in—*she types her number in*—and hands it back to me.

"See you tomorrow, Jack."

Cameron, his two buddies, and I all watch her walk away.

Cameron turns to me. "Jack Splat," he says a third time.

That's it. Nothing else. It's all he's got: name-calling. The lowest form of argument.

"Nice retort, dude," I say. I gather up my entrails and practically skip to lunch.

BAD STUFF SPILLING OUT IS GOOD

After lunch, me, André, and Joey Fillipelli are laughing and bouncing off each other like a trio of Ping-Pong balls. We pass Ms. Bennett in the main hallway.

"Mr. Acosta, can I have that minute with you now?" she asks. She adjusts her cat-eye glasses at the corner, and I'm not going to lie, it makes her look like a kick-butt supervillain.

Joey elbows me. "You're in *trouble*," he mutters.

"Uh, sure," I say to Ms. Bennett, and I duck back into her classroom. Classrooms have a creepy hollow feeling when they're not filled with breathing, sweating people.

I instinctively go to my desk, which is in the middle of the room. Then I realize how awkward that is, sitting there in the middle of all those empty desks with her at the front of the room. She must, too, because she perches on top of the desk two seats in front of mine.

"You didn't turn anything in today, Jack," she says. "On your project. I was really looking forward to yours, too."

I burn like exhaust fumes. I wait for her to continue, but she's not going to continue. How do teachers do that? Just sit there in all the uncomfortable silence? "I guess I don't really have much of an update," I say through my dry throat. Parched. Mummified.

"That's unlike you," Ms. Bennett continues at last. "You're usually a very good student. Your grades have slipped this unit, Jack. In fact, you're not passing this class currently. What's going on?"

Phoenix flashes through my mind suddenly. *Advocate for yourself.*

But instead, I feel anger burbling up inside me. Stage Two Decomposition: Gasses. Bloating. Discoloration. I respond more harshly than I expect to: "Nothing."

Ms. Bennett looks over the top of her red eyeglasses. Man, she really has this supervillain thing down. "You sure? Nothing going on . . . at home?"

Her eyes. It's the look I always try to avoid when

I'm out there scraping up guts: *pity.*

Rigor mortis hits. My jaw locks shut. My muscles clench. My nails dig into my palms.

How would she know what's going on at my home?

Does she really care that my dad moved out eight weeks ago?

Does it matter to her that my mom is obsessed with dead things? And I'm not really sure how healthy that is? That people think I eat roadkill? Or maybe that I just collect it for kicks like some kind of morbid Dr. Death? That they call me names like the Roadkill Kid and Jack Splat?

My Stage Two Decomposition *almost* morphs into Stage Three: active decay. In Stage Three, the cadaver reaches a point of rupture. Bacteria burst through the skin's surface.

I stand too quickly, and my desk chair squeaks extra-loud in this empty room. But I pull back on my anger. Rein it in to Stage Two. I force myself to smile through clenched teeth.

"Nope, all's good! Can I go now?"

Ms. Bennett stands, too. She looks at me like she did earlier, like I'm a specimen under a microscope. "Absolutely."

But she's standing in the same aisle as I am, and I can't get past without circling the whole room. So we stand there a moment longer.

"If you need anything, Jack, come see me, okay?"

Here's the thing about Stage Three Decomposition: Yes, it's messy. Very gross. Smelly. But when the fluids all spill out of a carcass, it's the beginning of what Dad and other soil scientists call the Cadaver Decomposition Island. CDI. The gross stuff inside spills out, and at first, it kills the grass and plants all around it. But then, it turns. It slowly makes the soil dark and rich and super fertilized, and the new grass is greener and healthier than the old.

Bad stuff spilling out is good, Dad would say.

I look Ms. Bennett in the eyes at last. "I will, Ms. Bennett. I promise. Thank you."

STOMACH ISSUES

It's rare that I get a stomachache so bad that I have to visit the school nurse, but after that chat with Ms. Bennett, I can't get my stomach to stop churning. The nurse's name is Ms. Ferguson. Some folks say she died long ago, and the *ghost* of Ms. Ferguson is actually the one who dispenses the Tylenol and Band-Aids.

"Do you want me to call your ma and she can come getcha?" she shouts.

"Nah," I say. "Uh, no, ma'am."

She squints at me and calls my mom to come get me.

On the ride home, Mom rattles, "We'll give you a couple of Tums, some water, you'll poop—"

"Mom! Gross!"

"What? Poop is natural. Best disposal system on the planet! You'll feel better right away, I bet."

We're in a line of traffic zipping down Highway 98, and I debate whether to tell her about my failing grade in Earth Science. That would likely help ease my stomachache. *Mom, that subject you love so much? Science? I'm awful at it.*

"Holy cow, is that a *fisher?*" Mom says. She slams on her brakes, pointing at a hunk of fur stretched on the side of the road. The car behind us blares his horn. Mom punches the gas but swings a hard left-hand turn into the parking lot of an old, abandoned gas station. No turn signal. The car honks at us again.

She spins a U-turn in the dusty lot and pulls out into the traffic headed the opposite way. "What's a fisher?" I say.

We pass the hunk of fur going in the opposite direction, Mom's eyes on it and not on the road. "It's like a mink. Or a ferret. They used to live in Tennessee a long time ago. Like, the 1800s—*that* long ago. But they were overhunted and went extinct in this area. Scientists released ten of them in Cumberland County in 2002. They've been trying to monitor them since."

Mom swings another U-turn in a church parking lot and heads back toward the roadkill. She pulls out too fast in front of the line of cars headed our way. The driver of the lead car gestures at us, and it's not a wave. My stomach sloshes.

"Adding a fisher to my data would be research *gold*! It would be research *dynamite*!"

Those two things sound like very different goals to me.

We zip past the fisher again, Mom muttering, "No place to pull over . . . Where . . . ?"

I strain against the seat belt, crane my neck, and press my forehead against the cool glass, trying to get a better look at this fisher. From what I can see, it's long and blackish-brown, with short legs and a weaselly face.

Mom whips into the gas station lot again. Then the church lot. She's circling this piece of roadkill like a buzzard. Her eyes scan both sides of the road, but there is too much traffic to pull over safely.

Mom smacks the steering wheel. "Darn!" she says, except she doesn't say *darn*. She drives past the roadkill, past the gas station lot, and we head home.

"A *fisher*," she keeps muttering, shaking her head.

My stomach flips. Nope. No way I'm telling her about Earth Science today.

At home, I plop down at the dining room table and look at all the Lego bricks I still have to lock together to finish this thing. The whole AT-AT is over 1,300 pieces. I've probably got 1,000 pieces to go. At least all the blocks are sorted by color. That's the hardest part.

Mom's in the kitchen on the phone again, obviously with Dad.

"*Five* days at Christmas? I don't think so, David."

"Well, because that's the end of the year. You know this. It's when the data for the grant is due. I can't—"

"*No*, I'm not saying I'm going to make him work over his winter break. Stop putting words in my mouth. But his help has been invaluable, and I . . ."

"I'm saying I can't do that much driving, David. Between here and your new place? Not then, not when I'll be crunching those numbers. Jack and I—we still live off that grant, you know. And the driving . . . we both know that'll fall on me."

"I said no!"

And then, silence. No goodbye, not even an "I'm hanging up now" like last time.

Silence is worse than a half-hearted goodbye.

I clear my throat.

"Mom," I call into the kitchen. "Want to come work on this with me?"

Mom shouts back, "What?"

"Want to build some Legos?"

Mom walks into the dining room and *immediately* steps on a Lego that's fallen on the floor. She hops around and says a string of words that'd make a sailor blush.

"Jack Acosta! It is way past time for you to clean up this mess!" she says at last, her face boiling red.

"But we—"

"Clean it *up!*" Mom shoves the dozens of piles of Legos to the other side of the table, messing up our sorting system. She stomps out. A mini Lego storm-trooper topples over on the table.

"Mom!" I shout after her. I look at all the Legos, now in one big messy pile of gray. The sharp corners stick out in all sorts of jagged directions. Like my mood suddenly.

22

I GUESS I SHOULD

Use a taunt here, Jack!" André leans far left in the beanbag chair, as if this will make Sonic the Hedgehog do what he needs him to do on-screen.

"Dude, I'm trying!" I say. I lift my controller, wires flying, hoping Link will do some showing off with that sword of his. We're furiously mashing buttons and fighting villains. Well, *I'm* mashing buttons. André is taking care of the villains.

The round ends. André's hedgehog break-dances, then does a forward flip as his point total goes up and up. André came to see me after school when he heard I wasn't feeling great. Pretty cool. And Mom let him in, even though I'm "sick." I think she was relieved to have someone else here as a buffer.

He grins at me. "Your dad is so much better at this game than you are."

"Tell me about it," I say. I flip through the character roster. Maybe it's time for Link to retire.

André sips a Dr Pepper and peers over the rim at me, like the soda can is a tiny shield. "You miss him?" he asks into the can. The question sounds small and tinny. "Your dad?"

I blink at the screen. It seems really bright all of a sudden. Yoshi—nope. Zelda—nope. Meta Knight—maybe?

"Maybe?" Why is my throat suddenly tight again? Like it was when Ms. Bennett was asking me all those questions earlier. "I mean. I guess I should."

"You *should*," André repeats quietly. He's not judging me. He's pointing out how odd that sounds—*I guess I should miss my dad.*

I feel Stage Three Decomposition churning my gut again. All the green, gassy goo burbling inside, wanting to burst out. It makes the tip of my nose sting.

Here's what I miss: my mom and dad telling stories together. They have so many great stories. Like the time they picked up a possum that was, well, *playing possum* and was not really dead. When they tell the story of that possum waking up in the back of the swagger wagon,

111

pushing the lid off the paint can, and dashing around the car shrieking as they try to pull over safely? They squeal and cry and laugh so hard it makes you think you'll pee your pants. Dad would say, "And *that's* when we learned"—and he and Mom would finish together, in tears—"you have to seal the can *every time!*"

When they share stories like that, you would think they fit together like "Once Upon a Time" and "The End."

As it turns out, they're just "The End."

And I'm the one picking up the dropped story lines Dad left behind when he ran away.

Whew. I am *not* going to do this now. Nope.

I pull it back to Stage Two. Keep all that ugly stuff inside.

"Yeah, I miss him. I hope I'll get to see him soon, though!"

I hear how fake my voice sounds. Like a taunt from an on-screen character.

André nods. We sit there for a minute. The only sound is the *click click click* of me flipping through the characters and the weird *whoosh* of the beanbag chairs. I desperately want to change the subject.

"Picked which comics you're going to submit yet? I'd still like to help." I say this without looking away from the clicking screen. I was kind of a dummy the last time we talked about this.

André's face lights up. "I haven't. Want to take a look?" He starts digging in his backpack.

I smile. It's so easy to make other people happy. Why do I always forget that? Just ask them about the thing that makes them light up.

André pauses and looks up from his backpack. "I've missed this, dude. Just us hanging out. No work. I'm glad I came by today."

I grin. "Me, too."

"You ought to be sick more often, then." He pulls a thick stack of paper from his pack, all with jagged confetti edges after being ripped from his sketchbook.

André spreads about thirty *Zombie Zoo* comics across my carpet. We're putting them in three piles— Yes, No, Maybe—when he looks at me side-eye.

"Zoe's house tomorrow, huh?" André says. He grins and waggles his eyebrows.

I burn as bright as the characters paused on-screen. Is this what lighting up feels like? "Yeah."

"You know what Jamal says about kissing."

I suck in a sharp breath. "I know what your brother says. He can't be right."

But André shrugs and continues: "Says it's just like eating a strawberry. That's what you do."

I'm shaking my head, but I say, "Do you really think

that's how it works? I mean, there's *teeth* involved."

André sighs and looks at the comic he's holding. "Don't know. But strawberries are pretty great."

"Yeah." But then I feel the need to add: "It's not like that, though. We're studying."

"Okay, boss." André grins as big as Sonic. A taunt. I shove him with my elbow.

We finish going through the comics. I've put like twenty of them in the Yes pile. Too many.

André laughs. "We can narrow it down again later. Let's get back to smashing."

I nod, pick up my controller, click through a few more characters, and find one at last.

"You're going with Minecraft Steve? Honestly?" André chuckles and shakes his head. "Okay. Let's do this."

"Let's do it."

I laugh, too, but my stomach is still filled with left-over churning goo. You can't just flip a switch and turn that stuff off.

Bad stuff spilling out is good, I think again.

But it's an awful, smelly mess, too. One I'm not ready to clean up.

HOME ALONE

Mom paces the house that night, the wooden floor-boards moaning every time she crosses the kitchen. *Eeee errr eeeep,* squeaks the floor.

She's sleepless again. Causing me to be sleepless again. The kitchen is right underneath my bedroom. I heavy sigh, flop onto my other side, and throw my pillow over my head.

She's mumbling and pacing, *eeee errr eeeep,* and then she stops.

Keys rattle.

Sccreeee-BLAM.

The back door?

I nod to myself. She's checking on her specimens.

She likes to do that to clear her head. Nothing like studying some unwound entrails to help you unwind.

But then? The car starts.

And the tires crunch down our gravel driveway.

Into the night.

She's left me here? I jolt out of bed, turn on my phone's flashlight, and stumble-race down the stairs. I pull back the heavy living room curtains and peek out the front window.

Into the night.

The glare of my phone's flashlight against the window throws my reflection back at me, and it looks like someone is outside, peering in. I shudder and snap the curtains closed.

Maybe she texted me where she's going?

Nope. Blank phone screen, throwing back just my reflection. Again.

I start pacing, and when the floorboard moans beneath my feet, *eeee errr eeeep*, I about leap out of my skin.

Where is she?

I skim the weak flashlight across the room into the kitchen. The shadows are long and tall and each one looks like an intruder. A monster. A wild animal.

At last, I see a note on the counter:

Jack, I couldn't stop thinking about that fisher. You

were sound asleep (ha!), *so I decided to go get it. A fisher! Be right back.*

I blink.

She left me alone in the middle of the night to go get roadkill?

A gust of wind pushes against the house. I jump.

"Okay," I mutter to myself, pacing, *eeee errr eeeep.* "She'll probably be gone about twenty minutes. That's not bad."

I crack my knuckles. "She's left me home alone during the day, right? This is the same thing."

I picture her on the side of a highway, in the dark, scraping that fisher off the road. The other cars will see her, right? They'll see her hazard lights? Swerve around her on that busy road?

Maybe it's not that busy at night. Maybe it'll be just her out there. All alone.

The shadows look like monsters.

My throat closes.

A tree limb scrapes against the living room window. My heart squeezes into my closed-up throat.

It was definitely a tree limb.

Was it a tree limb?

I squeeze my eyes shut. I can't pull back the curtain to check if it was a tree limb. I can't. I'll just find out for sure when the intruder takes a running leap through the plate glass window.

Has she left me before like this, in the middle of the night? And I never knew because I truly was sound asleep?

Stage Two burbles around inside me again. But this time, there's fear mixed in with the anger. Fury, I think this must be. I want to throw up. I want to scream. I want to punch something.

I punch a couch pillow. Very unsatisfying.

Do I text Dad?

I pull open our text thread, ready to type.

What do I say? Will this get Mom in trouble or something? Her voice was so angry and high-pitched when I overheard her talking to him earlier. Like she had been sucking in balloon air. The only times her voice does that is when she's talking to Dad about me. Fighting over me.

Weird things happen to kids in divorce. They don't know that I hear them talking about my split-up schedule and holidays and grandparent visits. Big fights and small jabs at the other parent that make me itchy uncomfortable. I don't want to make it worse. And I don't want to get Mom in trouble.

Gah! Why did they put me in the middle of all this?

When she gets back, I'm going to give her a piece of my mind. I'm going to tell her just how angry I am. When she—

Headlights sweep across the room, and gravel crunches under tires.

It's the swagger wagon for sure. No mistaking that big diesel engine. It sounds like a school bus.

The car door bangs. The wagon hatch bangs. Mom whistles and I hear the rattle of the chain-link fence, hear her enter the metal tagging shed.

About five minutes later, I hear the screen door open—*sccreeee!*

But before I even hear the *BLAM!,* I take the stairs two at a time. I hop into bed and throw the covers over my head. My heart pounds.

Mom climbs the stairs quietly, and I hear the soft *whoosh* of someone bending around my doorframe, checking on me.

"I got him, Jack," she whispers into my room. "I got the fisher."

She pads away. She didn't hear my racing heart?

I flop and punch my pillow.

Very unsatisfying.

SCIENCE IS ALL AROUND US

'm tired the next day from that restless night of sleep. I drop my backpack next to my desk, then drop myself into the metal chair. I take out my Earth Science book, and I *jump* because Ms. Bennett leaps into the room.

"Earthlings!" Ms. Bennett shouts. Wow—she is really worked up. "We have a special guest speaker today!" She bounds to her laptop and connects it to the overhead projector.

"I'm always talking about how science is all around us, right?" she asks while typing. It's true, she does. "Well today, we're going to hear from a famous scientist about how her work shapes our world!"

I sit back. Catch my breath. It'll be nice to have a change of pace today. A speaker rather than our circa-1999 textbook.

Ms. Bennett opens Skype, and a call quickly *bee-boo-boo-beeps* in. And there . . . THERE—ARE MY MOTHER'S NOSTRILS.

There's nothing up in there, thank goodness, but she's holding the phone at that mom angle, way down below. She's also walking, so the camera shifts between her forehead and chin, forehead and chin.

"HI, GUYS! THANKS FOR INVITING ME INTO YOUR CLASSROOM TODAY!" she shouts. I know I should be proud that my mom has figured out how to use Skype from her tablet, or, you know, that she's considered a very famous scientist, but I'm not. I'm dead. Newly deceased. Stage One Decomposition—body temperature quickly falling. Eyes glazing over. Tongue hardening.

"LET'S SEE, HOW DO I FLIP THE CAMERA— AH! THERE WE GO!" My mother continues to shout. She, like every adult I know who uses technology, doesn't trust the mic to pick up her voice. It doesn't help that she's covering the mic with her hand.

Mom flips the camera and there, splashed all over the wall in my Earth Science classroom, are our "pets"— Cottontail and Bob Ross and Nagini. Cameron squirms in his chair. "You gotta be kidding me!" he whispers to his cronies.

The cronies don't even chuckle in reply. They're too busy gawking at the roadkill in my weedy backyard.

I don't dare look at Zoe. Zoe, whose house I'm supposed to go to later today. No way she wants me tramping through her house now that she sees the mess my tennis shoes walk through every day.

My mom has on her blue plastic gloves, and she gently lifts the stiff paw of a dead groundhog. Chuckles. "YOU CAN SEE THE ROAD ABRASION HERE . . ." she shouts through Skype.

A girl across the room, I think her name is Amie, jolts upright and dashes out of the class. She is solidly green.

I am mortified. Which I happen to know comes from the word *mort,* which means *dead.* Of course I know that.

In my denial coma, I don't hear much else except words that my mom shouts here and there: "ENGORGED." "DISEMBOWLED." "FECES."

Cameron is laughing so hard he's twitching in his chair and tears are streaming down his cheeks. The rest of the room is so quiet you could hear a flea jump.

"BLOAT."

My eyesight fades to a pinpoint, and my hearing

sounds like I'm in a tunnel. This is it. This is when I pass out fully from embarrassment.

"FIELD TRIP."

I'm so dizzy I almost don't catch that last one. I swing my heavy head to look at George, behind me. He's mesmerized by what's on screen.

"Did she say *field trip?*"

George nods, never removing his eyes from the gore. "She said maybe in the spring we can do a field trip to see her research firsthand."

Cameron is chanting, "Field trip! Field trip! Field trip!" My mom and Ms. Bennett eat it up like flies on poop.

After eight thousand torturous hours of this, my mom shouts "BYE Y'ALL!" and Ms. Bennett sighs happily as the screen fades to black.

The bell rings, and it takes a second for everyone to remember that they're alive and needing to move along to the next class.

They file out. I don't know if they're looking at me or not. I'm gone, not here. I'm in another dimension altogether. Time travel via deep embarrassment.

When I come to, it's just me and Ms. Bennett. She's smiling widely at me. I blink in the neon lights of this classroom. I'm back?

"Please tell your mother thank you so much for

that amazing presentation!' Ms. Bennett says. "It fits right in with what we've been discussing: how wildlife shapes what the human world looks like. I'm beyond thrilled she volunteered to talk to our class today."

"Volunteered," I mutter, as I stumble out of the room. I'm supposed to go to lunch next, but no way is the Roadkill Kid showing up at the cafeteria today. I head to the courtyard instead. It's cold, so no one's eating out here. I suck in lungs full of sharp air. I'm alive. I lived through that.

My phone pings. I expect it to be Dad, but it's . . . Zoe? Here we go. She's canceling.

That was aaaahhhhhmazzzing. Your mom kicks butt. 4 o'clock today?

Another lung full of air, so cold it's like breathing knives. But I'm definitely alive.

I type back: **4 o'clock. See you then.**

Mom doesn't even sense the tension in the car on the way to Zoe's house that afternoon. She's bebopping along to some old George Michael song. *"Freeeeee- dom!"*

"Mom!" I bark at last. I click off the radio. "Why did you do that?"

Mom blinks. Does she honestly have no clue what I'm talking about? "Do what?"

"Gah!" I huff. We hit a pothole and the whole car thuds. "Why did you volunteer to talk to my class? About *roadkill*?!"

"Well, Ms. Bennett—"

"Don't ever do that again." I snap. "Don't ever invite yourself into my class without asking me."

I expected her to look hurt. Was I trying to hurt? But instead, she looks angry. Her lips are pinched flat and white.

"You've never talked to your dad this way," she says in a tone so level it gives me shivers. "So don't talk that way to me, either."

"Yeah, well, Dad's never volunteered to show disemboweled groundhogs to my entire class!" I growl. I turn as far away as I can from her while trapped by a seat belt. My forehead on the glass feels cool and damp. I breathe and the glass fogs over.

"Okay," she says at last. It's quiet, just above a whisper. "Okay."

I said what I needed to say.

Didn't I?

25

YOUR KINDRED SPIRIT

The doorbell at Zoe's house rings a long, fancy tune, like maybe Beethoven? Composers versus decomposers. Here in Zoe's world, composers win.

Zoe's house is monstrous, all stone and glass. It sits behind iron gates that buzzed open when we pulled up. It feels shiny and strong like a fortress. Very different from a weedy, overgrown farm that specializes in death and decay.

The heavy front door swings open, and Mom honks her horn just as it does. "I'll pick you up in two hours, Jack!" she shouts from the swagger wagon. I burn red like road rash. I wonder if Zoe can sense the raccoon in a bucket in the back, the one Mom made us stop and scrape on the way here.

After our fight, Mom tried to change the subject by telling me about that stupid fisher the whole ride over. *"They're special. They're rare."* Blah blah blah. She doesn't understand that lots of things are special and rare. Well—lots of things might not be rare. But lots of things are special.

And you keep those things close by. You don't chase them off.

Mom was able to get past our fight so fast. I'm still fuming. And the fact that she was able to *poof!* let it go so quickly angers me even more somehow. But I can't think about that now. I'm *at Zoe's house.*

"Sorry I'm late," I mutter at last to Zoe's fancy stone sidewalk. "Uh . . . traffic?"

I lift my eyes. Zoe is there, wearing a colorful shirt with butterflies of all sorts printed on it. And—

"Glasses!" I say before I can stop my mouth from saying it. Road rash again. "I, uh, didn't know you wore glasses."

Her green eyes are bigger and greener behind the gold round frames. I gulp.

Zoe's cheeks pinken. "Yeah. I wear contacts during the day, but sometimes when I get home I gotta take those things out." She pushes her glasses up the bridge of her nose. I grin. I try not to think about what stage of decomposition the flutters in my stomach equate to.

"Come on in," Zoe says. She leads me down a long hallway that echoes as we walk. Echoes! I've been in buildings that echo before—libraries, museums, hospitals—but never a house.

We go into a kitchen and there's a fire roaring in the fireplace. A fireplace. In the kitchen. We sit in two huge, cushy chairs and zip open backpacks.

"Jack, it's nice to finally meet you!"

I look up, and a woman wearing a head scarf and thousands of bits of shiny jewelry is smiling at me. She knows my name?

"Yes, ma'am," I say. I extend my hand.

"A handshake!" she sings. She clasps my palm with both of hers. Her hands are as soft and warm as I thought they'd be. No calluses from hefting a ten-pound groundhog with a snow shovel here.

"Can I get you two a snack?" she asks, and she *tings* and *clangs* as she swings around the island in the kitchen. She seems very different from Zoe's dad, the one who drives the Lexus and buttons his shirts all the way to the top. "How about some veggie straws?"

"Uck, *no*," Zoe says, rolling her eyes. "We're good, Mom. We need to get started."

"Don't mind me," she says. She drifts into the next room, but I can tell she's still nearby. I can hear her tinkling.

"So, uh, what animal did you choose?" I ask Zoe, flipping open my notebook. I didn't hear anyone else's choices after I spat out *cougar*. I'm trying not to look directly into Algebra-Green eyes. Avoid all stages of decomposition, Jack.

Zoe plops an open bag of Twizzlers onto the small table between us, and lays a finger across her lips, *shhhhh*. She lifts her chin at the doorway to the other room and smiles. Sneaky! I grab a red rope. Twizzlers remind me a bit of the ligaments that weave through muscles, binding them together, but I don't tell Zoe that.

"The starling!" she says, reminding me that I asked her a question. Her smile is like a star itself. "It's a bird—kinda iridescent purple with white tips on their feathers. Most folks call them an invasive species. They were brought to America in 1890 by some dude who was a huge Shakespeare fan. He wanted to bring all the birds mentioned in Shakespeare's plays to America. He started with sixty starlings. Now there's two hundred million of them in North America!"

She's so excited about these birds, and her joy is contagious. "Really? That's wild!"

"Gotta admire a creature with that kind of fight."

Zoe's mom clears her throat from the next room, which appears to be a dining room with a table so big, it looks like one knights would use. "Zoe, dear, we don't glorify fighting."

Zoe rolls her eyes but corrects herself: "Gotta admire a creature with that kind of staying power."

Her mom must be satisfied with that, because she starts humming and tinkling around the next room again.

"Tell me what you've found about cougars!" Zoe says. She sits forward, eyes sparkling, and I lose my train of thought for a second.

"Well, I—"

"Cougars!" Zoe's mom sweeps back into the room in a rush of colorful scarves and perfume. "Jack, are cougars your daemon?"

"My, uh, I'm sorry?"

"Your daemon. Your guide. Your oracle. Your kindred spirit?"

"I, uh—"

"Mom!" Zoe says. "We're trying to study!" Her cheeks are bright red now, hiding most of her freckles, but I laugh. Another person whose mom embarrasses them!

"Oh, I but must tell you about cougars as a spiritual guide!" Zoe's mom drags a heavy wooden chair across the floor and joins us. Zoe shoots daggers at her with her eyes. I can't help but laugh again.

"Jack, dear," she begins. Her face becomes serious. She talks with her hands a lot. "Cougars represent taking control of your life. Leadership. A boost of new energy. They represent courage, strength, and wisdom. But they also signal a need to work on self-confidence. A cougar signals you have been chasing the wrong things.

"Does this sound like you, Jack?"

The fire crackles in the fireplace. I blink. The next few seconds feel like an eternity.

"Uh, yeah. Yes. I guess it does."

"Mom," Zoe says with a hard edge. "We need to study now."

Zoe's mom's face transforms into a bright, cheery smile again. "Well, Jack. It's a delight to meet you. You've picked a great topic. *Bon chance.*"

She scoops up the bag of Twizzlers and tinkles out of the room, farther away this time.

Zoe leans back in her chair. I expect her to sigh, but she smiles and raises her eyebrows. "My mom can be intense."

"Oh, remember *my* mom?" I say. We laugh. And I have to say, our laughs sound good together, like peanut butter and jelly.

"Your mom is awesome!" Zoe lights up when she says this, so I don't think she's making fun. "What she does is just—wow!"

"Wow," I echo.

"I'd really love to have her come talk to my environmental club about women in STEM. And recycling! She's the ultimate recycler." Zoe has this far-off look on her face, like the idea of my mom speaking to her club is downright dreamy.

"She's the ultimate," I repeat. I guess I should be excited that all the gore earlier didn't scare Zoe away, but there's that thought again: Are we going to be friends just because of my mom? Because she's an environmental scientist? I deflate.

"My dad's a piece of work, too." She laughs. "An entire encyclopedia of dad jokes, that guy."

Dad. My stomach curls: Stage Two Decomposition. *Nope.* Not now. I chuckle. It sounds fake and cartoony. Like the emojis he's always sending me. "Ha. My dad, too."

Time to switch gears. I show her all the stuff I have on Phoenix so far. It's wild, but I'm not embarrassed to show her photos of tufts of hair and piles of scat. And Zoe is as fascinated by all this as I am.

"Jack! This is amazing! You've *seen* an actual *cougar*!"

I nod and grin. "I have."

"Lucky." Zoe sighs. "I've never seen a cougar before."

"Yeah, but they've seen you."

132

I *meant* that cougars are super sneaky, and they're closer than we think, and so they've probably laid eyes on her before. But I *think* it comes off sounding like she's one hundred percent, totally noticeable. Unmissable. Like I meant *me* and her and *gahhhh.*

I've resisted the stages of decomposition so well today! But now I am full-on Stage Five: Shriveled-up, dry remains. A skeleton. Bones.

"Do you have any water?"

Zoe leaves to get water, and I bite my lip. One thing I didn't tell her: what Phoenix did to Belle. I don't want her to think bad of Phoenix, like I'm protecting the cougar's reputation or something. I feel like I'm hiding a big, scary part of her personality by leaving that part out. Zoe doesn't know the whole story. I'm afraid of what she'd think if she knew all the dark stuff, too.

SOMETHING WE DON'T SEE
EVERY DAY

On the way home, Mom opens the windows of the swagger wagon. It's a cold early-December day, but our station wagon stinks in a way that few things do. Mom bleaches and scrubs and hoses it down regularly, but it still reeks.

I don't mind the cold from the open window. It pulls puffs of my breath into the sky. I wave my hand outside—up, down, up—as the car zips along. I'm happy even if I'm going to flunk. Even if my mom invites herself into places where she's not welcome. Even if she chases off things I love.

I'm going to fail Earth Science. Zoe agrees that I need more information on Phoenix the *animal*. Life cycles, territories, food-chain facts—that sort of thing. I know I can pad this report at the last minute, include all sorts of the cougar facts I dug up at the library, but honestly? I haven't looked up much on cougars after what happened to Belle. I'm nervous about what I might find. I don't want to be disappointed, I suppose. There are lots of things that I thought were really great in the beginning that turned out to be a big disappointment.

I practice it in my head: *Mom, about that cougar wandering around our yard: she's amazing but I can't seem to get past her terrible side and so I'm failing Earth Science okay bye!*

Mom inhales sharply. Did I say that out loud?

The swagger wagon swerves.

Grinds to a stop on the shoulder of the road.

Mom points and says breathlessly, "A coyote!"

Okay, normally I would be ticked that she's stopping for more road pizza, but a coyote isn't something we see every day.

Mom puts on her hazards, hops out of the car, drops the orange cones behind our vehicle, and we approach. She's already whistling, blocking off her nose, preparing for whatever stink coat this coyote might be wearing.

We're about five steps away from the coyote when Mom gasps again. She grabs my wrist.

"A collar," she whispers.

I blink at the hulking animal. Sure enough, around its neck: a bright orange dog collar.

It's not a coyote.

It's a German shepherd.

And Mom? She can't move. Frozen. Rigor mortis.

A low moan begins in the pit of her stomach. A single tear drops over the rim of her eye. She falls to her knees.

"Nooooooo!" she wails. She presses the heels of her hands deep into her eye sockets. "No no no no noooooo!"

My throat closes and my eyes sting. I look from Mom, who is wailing like a puppy who has lost its mother, to the dog, who is possibly leaving some puppy out there motherless.

I blink and blink and blink.

"Why?" Mom says. She pounds her fists on the gravel shoulder of the road. It has to hurt like crazy. "Why do people let dogs wander like this? Why do things die like this?"

All those worries that I've had recently, about my mom losing the line between life and death? About it being too blurry for her to see? She sees it, all right. She knows it's there. She sees the animal that once *was* from the shell they've left behind. She knows these

136

animals aren't disposable. She sees life lost. And that loss is pouring out of her eyes and her nose and her throat right now.

I don't want to make light of this injured dog, but I also need to get my mom off the side of the road. A trickle of blood carves across one of her dusty knuckles.

"Mozart versus mushrooms?" I say. My voice is shaky. I don't want to be near this dog anymore. It's too much. "We all know who's really the *fun guy*? The fungi . . ."

But my mom is still weeping. Still grinding her knuckles into gravel. She didn't even hear my stupid joke.

"Why are people so *awful*?" she shouts into the sky. The low December clouds absorb her punches like a pillow. "Why do they treat each other so *awfully*?"

I reach down and gently lay my fingertips on her shoulder. She looks at me, eyes red and nose snotty, and for a second, I am the adult and she is the kid.

I drop and hug her.

She hugs me tight—almost painfully so—and weeps onto my T-shirt.

I can't remember the last time I hugged my mom this hard or this long. It feels like a line that was blurry suddenly snapping into razor focus.

This is what the bad stuff spilling out looks like.

DECOMPOSED

Mom cries until her tears run out, then she pushes away suddenly and hops to her feet.

"Jack, check the address on that collar," she says, dusting herself off. She's ripped a hole in one of the knees of her jeans in the gravel.

"Why do I have to do it?"

We both turn to look at the dog. Maybe she's just sleeping?

Mom's eyes glass over again, and I shake my head fast. "No, no—I'll do it!" I snap.

I creep toward the dog.

Around the dog.

I've approached dead animals so many times. Why

does this one send chills down my spine?

I reach out and turn the face of the collar to me through her fur. It reads 2221 Smokey Hill Road.

It matches the number on the mailbox about twenty yards up.

I point at the house—a small cottage on lots of land. Mom's face turns stony as she stares at it. "I'm going to give those folks a piece of my mind," she mutters. "Letting their dog run free like that . . ."

I didn't look at the dog's name. I don't want to. I reach in my pocket and pull out the napkin I took from Zoe's house. It's recycled and has tiny wildflowers printed on it. I was using it to mop the sweat off my palms at her house while we studied. Now, I fold it gently, carefully. It turns out looking a bit like an origami flower. If you squint. I lay it down next to the shepherd. "Good dog."

I don't know this dog, but I know she was a good one.

Mom is already marching toward 2221, fists balled at her side. I have to jog to keep up. "Mom, listen. Losing a dog can't be easy. Maybe don't lecture them about—"

But she's ringing the doorbell already. The peeling-paint door swings wide, and a woman stands there in a muumuu. At least, I think it's a muumuu—I've only ever heard the word. But I imagine it looks like this shapeless dress.

She smiles wide, but her eyes are cloudy. Confused. "Hello, it's so good to see you again!" she says. I blink, shift my eyes to Mom.

Mom's stone face falters. "I, uh—"

"Won't you come in?" the woman says.

Mom shakes her head a bit. "I don't think—"

"Margaret!" a voice sounds from inside the house. "Just a minute!"

An older gentleman scoots up behind Mrs. Muumuu. He's wearing a trucker hat that says "Ernest Tubb Record Shop" on it. He smiles at her, puts his arm around her waist. "I'll take it from here, sweetheart."

She smiles at him, and her eyes lose their cloudy confusion. She turns back to us. "This is my husband, Matthew."

Matthew smiles at her. "Why don't you go into the kitchen for a bit?"

"I'll go into the kitchen for a bit."

Mrs. Muumuu shuffles away, and Matthew sighs heavily. Runs a wrinkled hand over his craggy face. "Sorry about that," he seems to say to the warped boards on the porch. "She gets confused." Then he remembers we're here. He smiles.

"How can I help you folks?"

Mom is staring after where Mrs. Muumuu disappeared into the shadows of the house. Then her gaze shifts back to this man. The woman's caregiver. Her husband. Her *till-death-do-you-part.*

Mom's eyes glass over once again. Her lips mash together, and she shakes her head.

She can't say it.

I clear my throat. "Sir, I think—"

My stomach and my heart are punching each other, fighting to leap out of my mouth. Why do I have to be the one to tell this man this awful news?

"Sir, I think something's happened to your dog."

I turn to gesture out to the road, to our car parked behind his I-wish-she-were-sleeping dog. I realize, suddenly, that I should add: "Um, it wasn't us. We found your dog like that. I'm sorry. I'm really sorry. I—"

The man, Matthew, has removed his dusty hat. He's clutching it to his chest. He takes a moment, like maybe he's muttering a small prayer. I wish like crazy he'd say his prayer out loud. I want to know how to do it. I want to know the right words to say when something crosses into the Big After.

When he opens his eyes, they are red but calm. He dabs at them with the backs of his veiny hands. He perches the hat high on his gray head.

"My wife. She forgets to close the gate."

141

Mom's tears are streaming fully down her face now, but she manages to eke out, "I'm sorry."

Matthew turns to her, gently squeezes one of her hands. *He's* comforting *her.*

"That old dog saw every opportunity she could to run wild and free," he says. "And who can blame her? I'd sure as heck run like that if I could!" He chuckles. "I learned a lot from that old girl over the past fourteen years. I guess her last lesson to me was: live life like someone left the gate open."

Mom smiles through tears.

We stand there a moment more, and it begins to feel awkward, like we're taking up space inside someone else's grief.

"I, uh, think we should go now," I say to Mom. She nods, turns, and walks silently down the porch steps.

Matthew extends his hand out to me. "Thank you for letting me know, son. You and your mom are good people."

I shake his hand. "Thank you, sir." But I'm angry and sad and confused. Stage Two Decomposition again: Churning. Bloat. When all that bacteria is fighting inside a dead organism to get *out.*

"You're quite the composed young man," Matthew says, still clutching my hand. Boy, his grip is strong. "Your parents. Good people." He releases my hand at last and closes the door.

I take my time getting back to the car. I know he means that as a compliment, *composed*. He means cool. Calm. Collected.

But it makes me feel angrier instead.

I don't *want* to be composed!

Doctors are *composed*.

Preachers are *composed*.

Principals are *composed*.

Adults are *composed*.

I don't want to be an adult. Not yet anyways!

I want to be a kid!

I want—

I want to be—

I want to be . . . *decomposed*.

THE OPEN GATE

Live life like someone left the gate open.
The air from the cracked windows in the car is
just plain cold now, not refreshing, so Mom rolls them
up. Cranks the heat. Which we rarely do in this car
because heat = stink. Closed up, shut tight. Stuffy and
stifling. Practically boiling.

Stage Two.

The windows begin to fog with our breath. Mom
hunches over the steering wheel to see out of the cloudy
windshield.

I haven't been living my life like that dog. Wild and
free. I've been an adult who still wears clothes from the
boys' department at Target.

I look at Mom, tired and tear-stained.

This is my open gate. I don't know what I'm going to find on the other side of the gate, what comes after the Big After, but it's time to find out.

Bad stuff spilling out is good.

It's time for Stage Three. Rupture. Ooze. Spillage.

It's time to decompose.

"I can't do it anymore! Mom, I can't be an adult and work so much and help you with your research. I can't. All this death and dying—I can't keep doing it."

Whew. It pours out of my mouth all at once, like when I open the gate those words have to be wild and free.

My nose is running and my eyes are leaking. Spillage. Wait—am I crying? But what was poison on the inside is growth on the outside. Dad always knew that.

Mom blinks.

Turns on her blinker.

Pulls to the side of the road.

Are we picking up roadkill *now*? *Gah!*

But I don't see anything furry. Red. Dead.

Instead, Mom drapes an arm over the steering wheel, lays her head on her elbow, and looks at me.

Looks at me.

She's not scraping or analyzing or chasing away. Just seeing.

It feels good.

"Oh, honey," she says. "I thought you wanted to help. I never would've *made* you help."

She's not crying. She's looking at me with clear, honest eyes.

I shake my head. "I don't really like being the Roadkill Kid."

Her cheek twitches. "The Roadkill Kid?" She's trying not to smile.

I mash my lips together, also fighting a grin. I nod. "Jack Splat."

She's smiling now, eyes twinkling, one eyebrow raised. "That's a good one."

"Mom!"

"The Carcass Collector. Guts 'R' Us. The Grim Reaper. King of the Vulture Culture. Oh! JACK THE RIPPER!"

"*Mom!*"

Mom and I are laughing. Laughing! It sounds like music. Like sunlight through clouds. Like the perfectly timed click of a camera lens. She heaves a big sigh. Leans back in the driver's seat and rolls her head, looking up at the car ceiling.

"You don't have to take on your dad's role for me, you know. I'm still getting used to how our family looks now, and you, of course, still have your dad. *Always.*

But his role when it comes to me? It just . . . goes away. It doesn't need to be filled."

She reaches over and tucks a lock of my longish hair behind my ear. "The role I don't want to live without is Jack the Kid. Jack the *Good* Kid. Jack the Son."

She blinks at me. "You need a haircut."

My eyes are suddenly all sting-y again. I blink and nod and clear my throat.

"Mom? I'm failing Earth Science."

She exhales. It's so cold in this car I can see her breath. "I know."

SOMETIMES THE HEALING HURTS

I get the irony of the Roadkill Kid failing Earth Science. I've seen earth turned inside out. I've scraped and sniffed and measured and bagged and tagged earth. I've seen insects and mushrooms and grass overtake a carcass and turn it back into earth.

Earth Science is my parents' jam, their livelihood, their bread and butter, and I'm failing it.

And Mom knew. She knew because Ms. Bennett emailed her. That's when the whole I-volunteer-to-speak-to-Jack's-class thing happened. I don't know why all that surprises me, but it does.

I tell her why, everything from the school project

to the wildlife website: "I picked *cougar* as the topic of my end-of-semester project, and I do want people to believe she exists. Because she *does*. You've seen it. She's healthy and intact and alive. And that matters."

I pause and try to think about what's bugging me. And I say it, *out loud*: "I'm like that cougar, I think. Me and Phoenix—all we want is to be seen, but it feels like all anyone else wants is to chase us away. You're chasing us away, Mom. You're chasing *all of us* away."

I can't believe I said it. Mom swallows hard. Her eyes glass over but she nods.

"But also, that cougar has so much darkness inside her. What she did to Belle . . . do we all have that inside us? She's so strong and mysterious and kinda scary? Am I like that, too? Why do I want to save something like that?"

Mom is quiet. We're back on the road and almost home. The pine trees lining the highway zip by in a blur. I expect that she's formulating a speech along the lines of *Those are just her instincts, Jack* or *That's how nature works*. And both are true.

"Jack?" Mom says at last. "You can't pick and choose just the good parts of someone. Or just the parts you agree with. When you choose a friend, or when you love something, you should try to love every bit of them. It's *so hard*, sometimes impossible, but you should try. Even the troublemaker needs love. Needs to be heard. Maybe more than anyone."

We're not really talking about the cougar anymore. I get that.

Mom winks at me. "You know, the troublemakers are the ones who make the history books."

I laugh. "Does that include the troublemakers who are failing Earth Science?"

She chuckles. "Definitely."

We're silent a moment before I say, "Mom?"

"Yeah?"

"Don't leave the house in the middle of the night anymore, okay? I . . . I don't like it."

We're in our driveway now. Mom puts the car in park and looks at me. She blinks. "Okay. I promise."

I think again of Phoenix, making her needs known. And I have one more, the biggest one of all. I suck in a deep breath and let it spill: "And Mom: I want to see Dad more often."

Mom is quiet a moment, but she says, "I think that's a good idea. He'd like that, too."

I'm happy but confused. All those fights, all that yelling, all those *different views of the world*—that doesn't just disappear: *Poof!* "I thought . . . maybe . . . he wasn't welcome anymore." Dang it! Am I leaking again? "Or maybe that *he* didn't want to see *me*?"

Mom stops picking at a hole in the car seat. Her eyes shoot up to meet mine.

"It's not you," she whispers. Her eyes get shiny, but she clears her throat and says again, louder. "Jack. It's not you. He is *always* welcome to be a part of *your* life. Please know that."

Wham. Just like that, I understand. *My dad left my mom.* She didn't chase him away, and he didn't run away from *me.* That hurts, but also? It kind of heals, too. No one ever tells you that sometimes the healing hurts.

How can something be both very hard to hear and exactly what you need to hear at the same time? I know my dad loves me. And I know my parents don't love each other anymore. At least, not in that till-death-do-you-part kind of way. In that Margaret-and-Matthew, Mrs. Muumuu–and–Mr. Trucker Hat kind of way. When I ask myself, *Do I even want my parents to get back together?* I know the answer: Nope. My parents are both awesome, but they're less awesome together.

Composers versus decomposers.

Mom smiles at me. Reaches over and squeezes my hand. "Want to go schedule a haircut?"

Lately, I've been worried about my mom and me. What we looked like without Dad. The Big After. Were we endangered? Officially extinct? I wasn't sure we even had a connection without him holding us all together like skin or tendons or ligaments.

But the two of us? Me and Mom. We're not extinct. Not even endangered. We're healthy and intact and alive. And that matters.

A NEW BEGINNING

The next morning, I head downstairs. I can feel my long hair standing straight, but I've given up trying to fight nature.

"Whew, I slept like the dead last night," I say to Mom, who stands at the stove.

"Ouch," she says with a chuckle.

"Too soon?" I ask. But I'm grinning.

"We all cope in our own ways." She's grinning, too. "Gallows humor, just like your dad."

Mom drops a cardboard box in front of me. "For you."

"What is it?"

"Open it and see."

I find scissors and cut open the tape. Man, they should use that packing tape in surgeries or to piece together tanks. That stuff is mega strong.

I finally get to the box-inside-the-box.

"A trail camera?" I look up at Mom. "How did you—"

"Very subtle hint, Jack. Leaving all those trail camera tabs open on my tablet."

I laugh. I hug Mom hard. "Thank you!"

She laughs, too. "I'll take the hug, but not the thanks. It's not from me."

I look at the shipping slip. "Dad?"

She nods. "Listen, bud. Your dad and me? We're not great together, but he loves you. So much. And he'll eventually figure out how to have a relationship with you again. He's figuring it all out, too, you know."

I had thought Dad was ready to be far from me and Mom both. Walk away without even a roadside memorial. Disposable.

But we're not disposable. Neither is he.

I rip open the trail camera box. This camera is *nice*: .4-second shutter speed, infrared flash, extra-long battery life, weatherproof (*duh*, I think when I read that feature), loads of memory. I can even transfer the photos and video straight to an app on my phone!

Plus, he must've shelled out the extra bucks to get

this thing here overnight.

I flip the camera back and forth in my hands. It's not huge—like three or four phones stacked together.

I text Dad: **Thanks for the camera! It's awesome!**

Dad writes back immediately: **You're welcome, bud! Happy early Christmas. Now go catch that cat!**

It's followed by a couple cat emojis, some paw prints, a camera emoji, and a poo emoji.

He knows all about Phoenix, and I haven't told him a word. Mom filled him in on all of it.

They have a Big After, too. It's *me*.

The final stage of decomposition is Stage Five, dry remains. Only bones and some fur and claws are left. But the grass and the plant life around the carcass are booming, tall and fresh and bright, because of the new nutrients in the soil.

A new beginning.

SAY CHEESE

Why do you keep bringing me out here in this murder forest?" André asks. The golf club is high and ready over his shoulder; his eyes scan the trees.

"I need you to be my lookout while I attach this camera to a tree."

"Well, pick one already!"

"It needs to be the right tree," I whisper. I don't know why we're whispering. It feels a bit like we're breaking into someone's house, coming back here in the woods behind our fence.

Our feet crunch in the leaves, over sticks. Only the pine trees bring green to this place. Everything else is a skeleton.

I'm looking at each tree carefully, trying to find one near the scat Phoenix left us a couple weeks earlier. Part of getting good trail camera photos is picking the right place for the camera.

"Dude, look!" André breathes. He swings his golf club and points to a tree trunk with the head of the club. "What is *that*?"

"It's a maple," I say sarcastically, but then I see what he means.

About four feet off the ground, the bumpy gray bark has been shaved off the outside of the tree in long scratches.

Claw marks.

I feel my insides light up like a video game bonus. "She's marked this tree! This is her territory."

André shivers. "Don't I know it."

I snap a photo of the claw marks with my phone. Man, I wish I had my real camera here. I wish it were easier to carry. These claw marks look like someone took a knife and dragged it down the tree, over and over.

I attach the trail camera to the tree just above the claw marks with the nylon belts that came with it.

I stand back.

"Say cheese!" I say. I wave.

The camera *clicks* with my motion. It works.

"Now what?" André whispers.

I gulp. "Now we get the heck out of here. Did you *see* the size of those claw marks?"

When we get back inside the house, Mom's in the kitchen, tablet in hand. She offers it to me. "Jack, today's rounds need to note how unseasonably warm it is."

The tablet hangs there in her hand, in midair. Heavy as a brick, that thing is. My eyes shift to André. He's frowning at the floor and nodding, thinking I'm going to ditch him again.

"I can't do rounds today, Mom." I gently shrug but my heart is pounding. Am I really doing this? "I promised André I'd help him with something."

André's eyes light up with his smile. "It won't take long, Ms. Acosta. I can help Jack with rounds afterward." He winces at the thought of what he's just offered.

Mom blinks. "No, that's okay. Too many people entering data leads to errors." Then, she does something weird. She *laughs*. It's been a long time since she's laughed on her own, without me making it happen.

"You know the saying," she continues. "Too many cooks in the kitchen spoils the broth." Mom licks her lips and waggles her eyebrows, like the thought of heading out to work on roadkill is *yummy*! She grabs a spatula off the counter. "Time to get cooking!" She opens the noisy screen door to the backyard.

As straight-faced as I can manage, I say after her, "Let's have Giggles for dinner tonight. It's been a while since we've had skunk stew."

"Oooh, yes," Mom says, hardly containing herself. "*Yum.*"

André makes gagging noises and shudders head to toe. "Nope. Nope!" He storms up our stairs. "Y'all are *wrong*. NOPE!"

Mom winks at me, and we laugh.

EVERYTHING ELSE

The next day, André and I stand in the teachers' lounge, which is always a weird place to be. It feels like accidentally opening your grandma's underwear drawer, walking in here. It's nothing you really want to see.

André removes a big orange envelope from his backpack. Inside are the top five *Zombie Zoo* comics we picked yesterday afternoon, over a massive bag of Skittles. It wasn't easy, but we did it. We narrowed it down to five.

André's drawn his two main characters on the outside of the envelope, screaming wildly, being chased by a whole parade of zombie animals. He's also written

"Ms. Sergio," the teacher who sponsors the newspaper, in big, dripping letters.

He finds the mailbox—Melissa Sergio—and slides the envelope inside.

We both stand there a second and look at it. Just sitting there. Waiting to make André famous.

I elbow him. "Dude. Congratulations."

André blushes. "C'mon, man. I haven't got the gig yet."

"No, but listen. You put yourself out there. You shared your work. Everything else"—I wave my hands around, as if André doesn't know what *everything else* means—"is out of your control. But you *did this*. It's brave, man. You should celebrate."

André lights up. "Sugar Shack?"

I smile but shake my head. "I can't. I've got to work on my project. It's due tomorrow." I kind of cold-sweat as I say that. Tomorrow!

André spins his Titans hat around backward. A rally cap. Baseball players do that when it's time to get serious. "Well. Let's get to work, then."

THE OPPOSITE OF DECOMPOSITION

If there was a competition for squirrel selfies, I would win. Those pesky little rodents are having a ball, performing for this trail camera. I have photos of squirrels smiling. Squirrels gathering. Squirrels laughing. Squirrels squabbling. I even have a photo that, if squirrels wore pants, this one would *definitely* be mooning me.

I swipe through the photos. I had no idea there was so much life behind our death garden! Deer and raccoons and birds and even an armadillo, trotting along jauntily. It's almost like I can hear his armor clanking when I see that series of photos.

Swipe. Squirrel.

Swipe swipe swipe. Squirrel squirrel squirrel.

Swipe. I gasp.

"Phoenix!" I breathe. "There you are."

In the photo, she's midstride, lifting her massive front right paw like it weighs a ton. I imagine it does. She's loping along, and her graceful tail swoops out behind her like a rope. That thing has to be over two feet long!

The tail makes all the difference. Getting a photo of that means I'll almost certainly get this photo included on the certified sightings list.

But the most stunning part is her eyes. She's looking directly at the trail camera, and her eyes glow like green globes, like tiny stars orbiting inside her skull.

"Whoa," André breathes. He's crawled out of the beanbag chair where he was sketching, and he's looking at Phoenix on the screen over my shoulder. "That is some cat."

"Isn't she?" I say with pride. I don't know why I should be proud—I mean, she's not mine or anything—but I still feel that way.

André nudges me with his elbow. "And those eyes. You got a real thing for green eyes, dude."

I'm sizzling red before he even finishes that sentence. I'm as obvious as a gang of turkey buzzards gathered along a roadside feast. *Sheesh!*

André flops back into the beanbag, and I gather all my Phoenix photos together:

A paw print.

A tuft of hair.

Belle the deer.

Some scat. Both intact and dissected.

Some scratches on a tree.

And her. Phoenix herself.

I describe and date each photo, and then I cross my fingers and hit send.

The *whoosh* of the photos being sent to the Tennessee Wildlife Resources Agency sounds like a big exhale. I flip through the photos of Phoenix again. Her looking right at the camera like that . . . it's almost like she's daring me to do something with this image of her.

Photographs are the opposite of decomposition. They are preservation. A moment captured, proof of existence. *I was* here, a photo says. And that lives on even past death. After the Big After.

The opposite of decomposition. Maybe that's why folks say you *compose* a photograph? Huh. For years, my parents and I have been joking about decomposers, and how they win every time over composers like Beethoven. But Beethoven's music lives on. Didn't he win, too?

I trace Phoenix's long tail on my computer screen. Even if I can't save *this* cat, these photos might help save other cougars.

That's what her eyes seem to say, the dare they lay out: *we are* here.

Photos like this seem to say: Death is not the end. There is a Big After.

I'm sure of it.

34

SMELLS LIKE ROTTEN EGGS

They should make trampolines out of the stuff they use to make these green plastic bus seats.

André and I bounce along down Highway 98, headed to school. Highway 98—I'm the only kid I know who can name all the highways and streets in the area. Chalk that one up to years of logging roadkill. I'm a regular Google Maps.

"Check it," André says, and he hands over his sketch pad. "New *Zombie Zoo*."

In the first three panels, our two main stars are being chased in circles by a zombie alligator. "BRAIIII-INNNSSSS," the alligator snaps. "GIIIIVEEE MEEE BRAAAAIIINNNS."

In panel four, the alligator stops abruptly.

Panel five: the alligator's lower jaw falls off, thudding to the ground.

Panel six: The three of them—two boys and the injured alligator—all stare at one another. The alligator looks particularly goofy with no lower jaw, all his upper teeth just . . . *hanging* there.

Panel seven: One kid turns to another and says, "Well, that was anticlimactic. Lunch?" Kid two says, "Yeah."

Panel eight: the two kids saunter away, leaving the goofy gator staring at his poor detached jaw.

A grin spreads over my face. "I wish my jaw would fall off so I didn't have to give this presentation today." I shiver.

"Naw, man. You'll do great. That presentation is fire. You have to deliver it *exactly* the way you practiced it."

He pauses then elbows me. "You told me yourself: putting yourself out there is brave. It's something to celebrate. You can't control anything else, but you can control *that*."

"Yeah." But my insides aren't so sure. My stomach churns like it's filled with mercaptan, a gas that accompanies decay. Smells like rotten eggs. Feels like a big ol' F on a project.

35

HERE WE GO

I am clammy and sweaty and my stomach churns. Back to Stage Two Decomposition. I bet I'm also bloated and green. Ms. Bennett adjusts her cat-eye glasses at the corner, where they are the pointiest.

"Okay, Earthlings. Any volunteers to go first?" she asks.

Crickets.

"I'm more lenient with my grading for those who go first, you know."

Cameron's hand shoots in the air. Ms. Bennett grins. "Mr. Talbott. Let's start with you."

Talbott. When I hear his real last name, I'm reminded that it's not too far of a leap to Totallyawful.

Cameron kicks the linoleum floor with the tips of his checkered Vans as he makes his way to the front of the room, *squeak squeak squeak*. Like a mouse.

He gets to the podium, clears his throat. Cracks his knuckles. Cracks his neck. Grips the podium. Leans forward.

"TheraccoonistheTennesseestateanimalitisthelargestmemberoftheprocyonidaefamilyitsgrayishcoathasa thicklayerofunderfurwhichprotectsitagainstcold weatherthreeoftheraccoon'smostdistinctivefeatures areitsfrontpawsitsfacialmaskanditsringedtail . . ."

I suck in a deep breath on Cameron's behalf. His report goes on like that for another five minutes, and I worry he might pass out. When he finishes, his buddies give him a standing ovation, and Cameron kicks one leg of the podium lightly, like a victory high-five.

"Thank you, Mr. Talbott." Ms. Bennett makes a few notes, then looks up at us again. "Who's next?"

I gulp hard.

My hand feels like it weighs eighty pounds, but I manage to lift it over my head. I figure going after that breathless presentation is my best shot.

"Ah, Mr. Acosta! Let's hear about your cougar."

Cameron and his cronies chuckle.

I make my way to the front of the room in a daze. Place my notecards on the podium. Look out at the millions and millions and millions of kids in my Earth Science class. The lights overhead buzz too loud, burn too bright.

My PowerPoint slides are washed out in this light. I hope they'll have the same effect. The slides are just rotating photos of what I sent to the Tennessee Wildlife Resources Agency, but I think they add a lot to my report.

My throat is drier than the bones in Stage Five Decomposition. Which is odd because the rest of me is leaking and sweating like I'm in Stage Three.

Why did I write my report like this? It's too weird. It's too different. I'm too odd.

I must be taking a long time, because Cameron fake-coughs loudly, and a few giggles pepper the room.

But then I see the best color: Algebra Green. I blink and focus on Zoe. She's giving me two thumbs-up. And when I focus more, I see she's wearing a T-shirt with a large cat striding across it, and the words "Cougar Truther" in rainbow print arching over it. She smiles, and it's like watching a shooting star.

I look at my notes and chuckle.

I *am* odd.

That's why I wrote my report this way.

I'm weird and different.

I am the Roadkill Kid. Jack Splat. A Cougar Truther.
I am DECOMPOSED.
I inhale.
Here we go.

THE REPORT

I have many names:
Cougar, mountain lion, puma, panther,
And not to brag or pander,
But I have forty more.
I have names galore.
In Appalachia I'm a catamount—a cat of the
* mountain*
A fountain
Of fright and awe—
With my one-inch claw, my four-toed paw
My hunger—
I am revered and feared.
Rightly so.

Apropos.
In the native language of the Alaskan Tlingit,
I am haadaa dóosh
A "surrounds-us cat."
I am that.
I sneak and slink and stalk
In wide circles I walk
Close, close.
My style is grandiose
But morose.
And my prey
Pray
That they
Never encounter
The vast array
Of my claw play.

We are the species Puma concolor—
"One-color cat."
My fur like cinnamon
Or cardamom.
But that—
the tone of my coat
the hue at my throat—
Is the very least
Of this beast.

I am misunderstood.

My tail can stretch three feet
A feat
That only the elite on feline paws
Can complete.
My tail helps me balance and leap
Creep and sweep and reap.
Into the sky,
I can fly fifteen feet.
Over the ground,
I can round thirty.
Strong legs and long tail
Help me curtail
The deer population.
For generations
I've hunted deer and doe
Blow by blow
Both high and low.
Low:
Where you used to live.
But you've moved UP.
I'm sorry we had to meet.

I am hungry.

You see
I need
One deer
Every sixteen days
To eat.
I devour ten pounds of meat in one meal.
Carving, consuming with zeal.
And then!
I hide the carcass,
Cover it with twigs and grasses,
And I save it for tomorrow
And tomorrow
And tomorrow.
I plan ahead!
Don't you see?
I'm so wise I surmise a future.
(If you'll let me have it.)
Deer meat
Keeps me alive
To thrive
To have kits.
Kids!
And with kittens
The meal supply must rise:
I need

One deer every three days.
To raise my young
To always
Amaze and praise my young
Like any good mother does.
But
I am running out of room.
I face doom.

I am crowded.

In the western states,
You build your homes
Farther up the mountain.
High, high
Close, close
You become
A surrounds-us human.
The deer now live with you.
And so I must, too.
But when I appear
To hunt my deer:
BANG! says your gun.
CRASH! says your car.
SCAT! says your voice.
Still you move and build

High, high
Close, close.

I tell you where my territory is:
I scratch a pile of twigs and leaves, called a
  scrape
Showing you how my territory takes shape.
I mark my home with urine and scent
Whittle trees with the intent
Of telling you: all of this is MINE.
And you call ME the intruder.
It couldn't be ruder.
I need two hundred square miles to call home
To roam
To hunt
My battlefront.
When you move in
To where I've always (always) been,
I have a choice:
Walk or stay.
I stalk away.

I am a newcomer.

I stride six states
To arrive in Tennessee

And here, I see:
I am still
Unwelcome.
"Extinct," you say.
You turn away.
And offer me no protection.
I feel your rejection.
Will you look in my yellow eyes
And deny
I exist?
I am a ghost of the wild.
I am mild.
I am meek around humans—
You are more likely to be struck by lightning
than attacked by me—
But I am far from free.
I could die away
In fifty more of your birthdays
If you continue to look the other way.

I am endangered.

I can live to see eight or ten years.
What kills me?
Cars.
Poison.

Other lions.
Hunters.
In other words:
Humans.
Humans.
Nature.
Humans.
I am a mystery.
Throughout history,
People want to see me
But they flee me.
Yes, I am endangered.
But YES.
I am here.
Do you hear me?
You ARE near me.
And
I AM HERE.

THE ROADKILL KID AT THE SUGAR SHACK

The seats in this diner are an awful lot like the seats on the bus.

But I don't mind it here.

Because the universe's best freckles dot the booth across from me.

"I bet a lot of kids in that class will start looking for cougars now, don't you think, Jack? I bet they'll check out that website and try to get a photo on there, too. I want to!" Zoe is rambling and I'm grateful she is, because then I don't have to say anything stupid.

"You should've seen him, André," Zoe continues.

"He looked like some artist in a café on slam poetry night. Rather than, you know, our smelly middle school."

Stage One Decomposition is "fresh." The heart stops beating, a stable body temperature is no longer maintained.

That's me. Now. In this diner with Zoe as she gushes on about my report.

"Even Cameron told him his report was cool," Zoe says with a laugh. "And Cameron doesn't think anything is cool. Well, except himself."

That was something, Cameron telling me that after class. Roadkill and Cameron have something in common—neither is disposable. I mean, neither is ideal, but each can be useful in its own way.

André smiles around the straw he's using to drink his peanut-butter-and-marshmallow-fluff milkshake. "Dude. You aced it." He holds out his fist.

I slurp up the last of my chocolate malt and grin at the cherry in the bottom of the tall glass. "I did. I aced it." I bump André's fist. *Boom.*

Zoe bounces on the seat across from us. "Can I come look at the other trail camera pics sometime? Those photos were awesome! I wonder if my parents would get me one of those?"

"Uh, sure," I say. Under the table, André is stepping

on my toes every time Zoe compliments me. It feels as obvious as cow roadkill. (Which I've only seen once, but it's *very obvious*.)

Zoe lists off the dozens of things she'd look for with a trail camera: ". . . and possums and raccoons and, oh! Snakes . . ."

André's eyes dart back forth between Zoe and me, and he's grinning like he's trying to stitch us together, like some kind of weird cupid. I'm burning as hot as a tar road in July, so I look around the diner.

This diner. The Sugar Shack. I'm finally here. Mom and I don't eat out very often, and she'd never choose a place like this. It's bright and has a loud jukebox in the corner, and the waitress smacks gum in your face— it's all part of the schtick. Zoe wanted to treat me to a milkshake after my report. Mom replied to my text with a **Sure! Have a great time, sweetie!** I don't know why that surprised me, but it did.

She meant it. I need to be a kid. I smile at that cherry again.

"Hey!" André says when Zoe takes a breath. "Want to see the latest *Zombie Zoo* comic?"

"A comic? Yes!" Zoe says, and the smile that I didn't think could grow any bigger grows bigger.

"You showed it to me this morning," I say.

"Naw, dude," André says, fishing around in his

backpack. "The *latest* latest."

I laugh as he flips open his sketchbook to, yep, a new comic. "That was fast."

André shrugs. "What else am I going to do in Algebra?"

I flip the sketchbook sideways, so Zoe and I can both read it. She tucks her knees under her and leans over the table, her fox-colored hair flopping over her face. I gulp and read next to her.

Panel one: An entire army of zombified animals marches toward our two shivering, huddled main characters. There are zombie flamingoes. Zombie rhinos. Zombie kangaroos. You name it.

Panel two: They march closer, shouting "BRAAAAIIINNNSSSS." The two humans hug each other tightly, eyes squinched shut. "Noooooo!" they say together.

In panel three, the gap closes.

Panel four: One tiny bug appears in the corner. An arrow points to it, and words above label it a "dermestid beetle." The bug has one fist on its hip, another jutting into the sky. "I'll save you!" the beetle declares. (André drew the specch bubble here really big and the words inside really small.)

Panel five: The beetle puts two buggy fingers in the corners of his mouth and whistles as the zombies trudge

183

ever closer to the two terrified humans.

Panel six: An army of dermestid beetles appears and goes head-to-head with the zombies.

Panel seven: The beetles plow over the zombies, all teeth and chomp. They're devouring the zombies. The words *BUZZZ!* and *MMM!* and *YUMMY!* spring over their buggy antennae.

Panel eight: The zombies collapse in a pile of bones. The beetles lie around, gripping their full bellies and griping, "Ugh! I'm *so full.*"

Zoe laughs. André stomps my toe. I smile. "One of your best yet. That one for sure would've made the cut for the *Gazette* contest."

Zoe's eyes widen at André. "You're doing that? I'm on the paper. I'll put in a good word. Your stuff is great."

André grins. "That'd be awesome—thank you!"

Zoe and André start talking comics and comic books and Marvel versus DC. ("Marvel. *Duh.*") I trace a fingertip over André's art.

Zoe wiggles her fingers in front of my face. "Helloooo, Jack! Are you in there?" Then, to André: "Does he always space out like this?"

André chuckles. "Yep."

Zoe whacks my arm gently with the back of her hand. "I *was saying*: I want to talk to you about the next environmental club meeting."

Ah. Here we go. I knew it. Zoe wants to be better friends because of my mom. I nod. "I'll see if my mom can make the next meeting."

Zoe's forehead crinkles in a way that makes me think of gift wrap. "No, I want *you* to give your cougar presentation. The members will love it!"

André is stomping my foot so hard I'm surprised the bones don't crush. I bite my lip to rein in a massive smile. "Yeah, uh, that'd be great."

Zoe nods once. It's settled. She and André go back to discussing comics. I go back to running a fingertip over André's tiny cartoon beetles.

André is disgusted by these beetles, and he found a way to make them the good guys. I think that's what my mom is trying to do, too, with her roadkill. My dad and his new single life. Zoe and her environmentalism. Me and cougars.

We all want to find a way to turn something awful into something good. Turn carcasses into dark soil where big, soft roses bloom.

38

ENOUGH DEER

A ninety-eight! Jack, that's amazing!" Mom smiles at the curvy highway ahead of us. She sneaks a peek my way. "Why wasn't it a hundred?" She winks. "I'm kidding, of course. You know I don't care about that."

She is. Mom's mantra when it comes to grades is: *Did you do your very best? Did you give it your all?*

"Ms. Bennett even wrote the TWRA to encourage them to post my pictures."

"She's a good egg, that teacher of yours."

Good egg. Where do parents even get this weird stuff?

"But listen," Mom says. She takes a deep breath. "Now that you've got the photo of your cougar and your project is done, I have to install some bright lights back there. Maybe a motion-sensor alarm, too. Our cat is cool but she needs to find a new home. Our specimens . . ." Her voice trails off. "Chuckles and Sparky and Rosebud . . . we can't lose them, too. Understand?" Mom bites her lip. She's worried I might be upset.

I am, a little. But Mom used the nicknames I gave to our "pets"! She's never done that before. Maybe she'll even start calling them our "pets," too. That would be something! And hey: Phoenix has come this far east. A little farther and she'll hit the Smoky Mountains. That will be paradise for a catamount like her. "I understand."

Mom's phone rings, and she waves her wrist at it. That's my sign to answer it and put it on speaker phone. (The swagger wagon doesn't have Bluetooth. The swagger wagon doesn't even have electric door locks.)

I answer, and Mom shouts, "Hello?"

"Jen?" a gruff voice shouts back. More shouting. Seriously. Adults do *not* trust that their tech will pick up their voices. "Hey, it's Walt."

Walt is Sheriff Bowling. He and Mom went to high school together.

"All good, Walt?"

"Yeah, listen. We got a deer down here on McMinn Road. Big fella—five points. Clean hit, too. I'd rather you get this one than see it end up in the landfill."

I sigh, but I ready myself. A five-point buck is a big deer. Huge. Hard to pass up a specimen like that. We need to at least see if we can manage getting him home. We might need to borrow Ms. Zachary's flatbed trailer for this one.

"I can be there in five," Mom says, checking her rearview mirror. She swings a wide U-turn and we head back toward McMinn.

Sheriff Bowling has his lights on behind the massive deer, and he's waving traffic around it. Mom pulls up behind him, and I drop the orange cones behind our car.

The sheriff hugs Mom, then puts on a stern face. "You know the drill, Jen. Gotta see your permits."

"Yeah, yeah," Mom says, but she's smiling. She digs in her purse, pulls out a bunch of pink and yellow forms.

The sheriff chuckles. "Because remember the confusion that time Joe pulled you over and you didn't have your permits."

Mom laughs. "How can I forget? Thought I might spend the night in jail."

"What?" I say, looking between my mom and the sheriff. "Jail? I need to hear this story."

Mom smiles and snaps on her blue plastic gloves. "Let's just say this—when you're pulled over at night and you're covered in blood, you better have your road-kill permits with you, or there will be *lots* of questions." Mom and Sheriff Bowling laugh.

"Uh, I need more details?" I say with a grin.

Mom gets this misty look on her face—not like she's about to cry. More like she's watching a movie from the past.

"Ask your dad to tell you that story," she says at last. "He tells it better than I do. It's a hoot."

I smile. She's giving Dad this one. It's been a long time since she's done that.

Mom circles the buck. She squats and tilts her head. She shields her eyes from sunlight. She pries open his lips, his mouth, and she pinches his tongue—it's still soft. This is a newly departed buck. Once the tongue hardens, it's all downhill from there.

Mom gently lifts an eyelid. The buck's eyes are open, but she's checking to see the state of the eyeballs. Eyes tell a lot of the story. These eyes aren't milky, haven't yet clouded over. They're barely dilated. This is a *very* newly departed buck. Probably not even an hour has passed since he . . . passed.

Then, Mom ever-so-lightly touches his antlers. They're huge and strong, and they make my heart hurt a bit.

I *don't* want to move this massive hunk of meat, but I think of Phoenix and shrug. Maybe she'd visit again one last time for this big fella? I know we're supposed to chase her away, but it'd be nice if she'd drop by once more.

Mom whips out her phone and punches in a few numbers. I figure she's calling Ms. Zachary for that flatbed.

So I'm surprised when I hear a voice through her speakerphone shout, "Hunters for the Hungry. This is Jason."

"Jason!" Mom says. "It's Jennifer Acosta. Listen, I got a buck that I think your organization could put to better use than I can right now."

They talk for a bit longer, and I'm as stunned as, well, a deer in headlights (too soon?). Mom is giving this deer to an organization that will use it to feed hungry people.

She hangs up, discusses a few things with Sheriff Bowling, then walks back over to me. She picks up our cones, then tousles my hair.

"New haircut looks good. You ready, kiddo?"

"We're really leaving this deer behind?" I ask.

Mom nods. "We have enough deer."

I laugh. Because what I heard was *We have enough, dear.*

And I agree.

Mom and I? We're here, in the Big After. The A.D.

timeline: After Divorce. We may not know what's next, but at least we're facing it together. What feels like the end is never really the end.

The end!

We're just about to leave the scene when it hits me: "Oh! Wait a second, Mom."

I leap out of the swagger wagon, dash past Sheriff Bowling, and scan the roadside.

That big branch. It looks like antlers.

I drag it near enough to the deer to be a memorial, but far enough off the road to be safe. The sheriff narrows his eyes at me but doesn't ask questions.

I leave the branch in a ditch next to the deer. I know at last what to say.

"You lived life like someone left the gate open."

I NOTICED

I fish deep in the pocket of my cargo pants and find the Dove chocolate I got for Mom. I leave it by the coffee pot—she likes to drop them in her cup. I traded Joey Fillipelli three peanut-butter cookies for this one.

I swing under and into my new camera strap. The camera hanging around my neck feels sturdy and safe and right, *comfortable*, like a weight I was always supposed to carry and didn't know it.

The neck strap was a Christmas present from Mom. When I opened the shiny Star Wars paper, she said, "I noticed you've been taking a lot of photos with your dad's old camera lately. You need a strap to carry it."

The best part of that gift? Her saying *I noticed*. That's a weight I don't have to carry anymore.

The other cool Christmas present Mom got me was a new Lego kit: Kylo Ren's shuttle. It's awesome! We worked on it together Christmas morning, before I went to Dad's apartment for the afternoon. That was weird, but it wasn't terrible. Not as awful as I thought our first Christmas apart would be.

As we were sorting the pieces, Mom said, "I think I love Legos so much because sometimes it's nice to build something, rather than watch something waste away."

I agreed.

Ping!

A text pulls me out of that memory. Gotta be Dad. Not many people text me. André and I message through WhatsApp, and Mom only responds to texts. She never starts them.

But it's a number that was added into my phone just a couple weeks ago.

Zoe.

Hey! Just saw some roadkill on the side of the highway and thought of you lol

Followed by a skull emoji, a squirrel emoji, and a big red question mark/exclamation point emoji.

I laugh. Emojis are awesome.

THE END (IS NEVER THE END)

AUTHOR'S NOTE: I'M A COUGAR TRUTHER

An estimated one million animals are killed by cars each day in the United States.

That is a *lot* of roadkill.

Most roadkill is directed to landfills and dumps, but because there is so very much of it, scientists, artists, and other visionaries have begun trying to see roadkill in a different light. It's human nature to try and take something bad—a true problem like roadkill—and turn it into something good. And some of the solutions for roadkill are very creative.

Yes, some people find, clean, and eat roadkill. You must have a permit to do this, and those who do this are usually experts in hunting and trapping already. (The Tennessee Wildlife Federation does indeed operate an organization called Hunters for the Hungry, and while their focus is on donating meat they've hunted, like venison, I imagined in this story that some of the "cleaner" roadkill might work for this program as well. Hunters for the Hungry provided over 569,000 servings of healthy protein to Tennessee food banks in 2020. Amazing!)

The state of Alaska claims all roadkill as property of the state, and they use much of it to feed hungry families. Other solutions for using roadkill: The states of New York, Virginia, and Maryland all compost some of these carcasses, making rich soil for things like roadside wildflower projects. In Missouri, roadkill is brought to bird sanctuaries and the Endangered Wolf Center, and they use the meat to feed the animals that live there.

And individual roadkill collectors help, too. One fashion designer uses road-killed fur in her clothing line. Some roadkill is taxidermized and transformed into art. (I read of a foosball table using taxidermy mice and squirrels as the players?!) Skeleton articulators, like Odette in the story, also "repurpose" roadkill. (An excellent graphic novel featuring a skeleton articulator is *Snapdragon* by Kat Leyh.) Skeleton articulators clean the bones of roadkill and sell the skeletons online, or donate them to museums, or use them for study.

Study. That's where the real meat (too soon?) of roadkill lies.

Heather L. Montgomery, author of *Something Rotten: A Fresh Look at Roadkill*, understands the importance of studying these animals. (Heather's book is a must-read for budding scientists and roadkill enthusiasts. If you love gobs of *aha!* and *what?!* and *ooooh, gross* moments while reading, *this book is for you*.) Studying roadkill can help us better understand everything from decomposition cycles to soil composition, from animal disease transmission to DNA models, from traffic patterns to animal migration patterns. Studying roadkill gives us insight into animal population trends, species distribution (in other words, where animals live currently), species invasions (like armadillos and cougars in Tennessee), and how contaminants (chemicals and poisons) build up in an ecosystem through the food chain. Studying roadkill makes us smarter and safer.

Safer, for both animals and humans. When there are over one million animal-versus-car collisions each day, that's a lot of car damage and, unfortunately, human injury. Studying how to reduce these types of accidents not only saves animal lives, but also human lives. If you're passionate about learning how to help, research *wildlife bridges*. These bridges help ease animals over (and sometimes under!) major highways, and many wildlife experts are lobbying for them to help decrease roadkill numbers and guide animals toward safer territories. (A great book on this topic is *Cougar Crossing: How Hollywood's Celebrity Cougar Helped Build a Bridge for City Wildlife* by Meeg Pincus, illustrated by Alexander Vidal.)

Another way you can help roadkill researchers is by serving as a citizen scientist and logging the roadkill you encounter. iNaturalist.org is a website and an app that has been tracking roadkill since 2013. The website says: "This project is designed to document as many animals killed on public roadways as possible. Only take photos if doing so will not endanger you or others. Information sought: Sex of animal, location, estimated time since animal was struck, type of habitat on each side of road." If you live in the UK, you can report roadkill on projectsplatter.co.uk (but anyone can follow them via social media and see what they call their weekly #roadkillreport. It's fascinating! They are on Twitter and Facebook as Project Splatter.) In fact, according to globalroadkill.net, there are currently a number of different roadkill reporting schemes worldwide.

One of the most fascinating roadkill studies I read highlighted the Burmese python in Florida. The Burmese python is an invasive species there, meaning they aren't traditionally a part of the ecosystem. Experts believe Burmese pythons became a part of the Everglades ecosystem due to two factors: irresponsible pet owners releasing their snakes into the wild, and hundreds of snakes escaping a python breeding facility during a treacherous hurricane. (Yep, that happened!) These snakes adapted quite easily to this new ecosystem, but the ecosystem is now highly unbalanced. One roadkill reporting study now shows a 99.3% reduction in raccoon roadkill—99.3%! We now know because of this roadkill study that raccoons are one of the python's favorite snacks.

One study, titled "The value of monitoring wildlife roadkill," written by Amy L. W. Schwartz, Fraser M. Shilling, and Sarah E. Perkins and published in *The European Journal of Wildlife Research*, says this: "In many ways, roadkill observation is likely to become the most useful single wildlife observation and sampling approach available for ecology." In other words, studying roadkill is the most useful way to learn about animals and their habitats.

As for cougars migrating to Tennessee: a Tennessee wildlife removal organization includes this quote on its site: "[The] head within the sand position flies within the face of decades of evidence. . . . The regulatory office of natural resources has ignored eyewitnesses, scientific studies, videotapes, still photos and requests for assistance from citizens and law enforcement agencies and animal control officers. The regulatory office of natural resources has stated that it has discretion under the endangered species law to do nothing about mountain lions . . . [This] stance might be irresponsible, and the long history of mountain lions within Tennessee might be compelling. It's now time for legislators to put an end to bureaucratic stonewalling."

While I could not find a direct attribution for this quote (in other words, who said this originally? I'm not really sure!), I wanted to include it because it says exactly how I feel about the possibility of cougars in Tennessee: it is irresponsible of us to ignore the facts. Cougars within a state's borders should be protected and (perhaps more importantly to our safety) monitored. To ignore their presence will harm us in the long run.

The information that Jack finds online about cougars in chapter 9 is actual information found on the website maintained by the Tennessee Wildlife Resources Agency. You can find this information and more at https://www.tn.gov/twra/wildlife/mammals /large/cougars.html.

Also, if you'd like to see the current list and a map of confirmed cougar sightings in Tennessee, visit that same link above. One of the coolest entries in the list says, "Hair sample was submitted by a hunter; DNA analysis indicated a female with genetics similar to cougars in South Dakota." South Dakota! That's 1,100 miles from Tennessee!

As for me? I'm a Cougar Truther. I live in Tennessee, and I believe they are here. I've never seen a cougar, but I believe they've seen me.

My thanks to the amazing scientists and authors doing research on things like roadkill and cougar migration so that we can better understand and aid the world we live in. Any errors in this story are mine.